BITTER BREED

DINO PARENTI

JOURNALSTONE
YOUR LINK TO ARTIST TALENT

ISBN: 978-1-68510-136-7 (tpb)
ISBN: 978-1-68510-137-4 (ebook)

First printing edition: September 27, 2024
Printed by JournalStone Publishing in the United States of America.
Cover Artwork: Don Noble
Edited by Sean Leonard
Proofreading, Cover Layout, & Interior Layout by Scarlett R. Algee

JournalStone Publishing
511 Deer Lake Drive West
Carbondale, Illinois 62901

JournalStone books may be ordered through booksellers or by contacting:
or
JournalStone | www.journalstone.com

"To think the way you do, you have to be a man who lives either on a tremendous despair, or on a tremendous hope. Or on both perhaps."

—Albert Camus, *A Happy Death*

BITTER BREED

1

THE HORIZON UNPEELS in slow increments of salmon and marigold against the jagged pinnacles of the Canadian Rockies.

Amos watches the dawn sun heave itself in real time, arm stretched across the rear headrest of the RAV4, cheek nestled into his shoulder. More a child's attitude than a middle-aged man's. Though not intentionally admiring the sunrise, it is directly in his view through the rear windshield and quite stunning in its alternating light and darkness. Clouds dense and sooted with snow absorb the brimming flush of morning along their crenellations, evoking a brain glimpsed as its negative on film. What his upright progenitors must've wondered of such a sight, he thought. What portents and fears. But it's not natural beauty he's scanning for. Like his ancestors, he's looking out for what may or may not be stalking them, even fifty miles and two hours removed from the source.

Up front, Doug and Vera sit in unbroken silence, the former driving mechanically along mountain hairpins and switchbacks. He knew Doug had grown up in the Rockies, and whether a conscious thought in the moment or not, Amos had told him to drive—his own muscle-memory cured through various military endeavors trusting in Doug's to get them up the ridge through his and Vera's bingo-cage tumble of emotions. The shock will knead them for a while still. They're scientists in their late twenties, unacclimated to bloodshed and death, especially when it's wholly unexpected. Likely the logic centers of their brains are, at the very moment, trying to shimmy through the morass, reassuring them, rightly or wrongly, that distance is now their ally.

Watching the sanguine light creep behind them, Amos isn't at liberty to feel so sure about that. He shifts some to keep his extended arm from falling asleep, and the slight movement is enough to send pain stabbing up from his leg. He didn't even know he'd been wounded until someone running past him in the lab cited the blood pooling around his shoe, barely hearing the words over the klaxons. The rest went down too fast to cobble any cogent narrative from but for glimpses. Blurs of movement too quick to characterize. Flashes of gore and bodies writhing or motionless. Sounds of crashing and upending. Of praying, blubbering, and screaming.

Get to a vehicle and get over the mountain was all his instincts barked for—reflexes that likewise snagged a panic-frozen Doug and Vera along with him. A childhood of repetitive study and testing off all imaginable charts had wrung his developing mind of the more normal, languorous experiences of youth for flurries of preparation and execution. But some drive for communion still survived the voyage. Perhaps it ran deeper for him than these two just being his underlings and cohorts. Perhaps greater emotions had imprinted and acted out in the moment that he wasn't yet ready to dwell over and comprehend. Whatever the rationales, they've culminated in the three of them sluicing between scrims of aspens and cedars in the Yukon, heading away from death and toward whatever the mountains held in wait.

For another ninety minutes, no words are spoken, no sounds exist but for the crunch of tire on snow and the fifing of wind through a window not fully settled within its rubber channel. At some point they round a bend and Amos, on a fortuitous stretch in which he stares ahead between Doug and Vera through the front windshield, sees a structure come into view.

At the node of a mountain hairpin, sheltered within a crescent of canting white spruce and lodgepole pine, a diner.

Last Chance Grill, says the sign—a chrome glass block, a pastel-hued relic from another era and nation.

They *should* keep driving, the rational half of Amos's brain insists. Summit and descend to the other side of the mountain and the warmer valley. To Fort Greely, where they can regroup and find help.

"Pull in here," his hastier half says—the part of himself he's let free-range more of late, and which may have led them to their current predicament, though he's not ready to concede anything yet.

Doug and Vera's heads slowly twist to Amos in a perfect mirroring each other. Their slack jaws and wandering eyes tell him all he needs to know.

"We should sit and strategize. Give the engine a break."

He doesn't say that *they* need rest, nourishment, hydration. That they're likely about to hit the wall emotionally, and Doug trying to negotiate icy mountain roads downhill while fighting the shakes won't do anybody any good.

The two up front connect eyes for a moment, whereupon some primal accord is shared, and slowly Doug coasts the vehicle to a stop across the road from the Last Chance Grill.

2

"GOVERNMENT?" SAYS THE large police officer in a well-deep monotone. His name tag reads *L. Denton.* For someone of his size, he sips on a London Fog in the dainty manner of British cozies, whipped cream gilding the bottom of his walrus mustache.

The other officer—P. Gaboury—takes a pull of Coke from a bottle, swishes it like mouthwash, and vaguely shrugs. He passes a hand across his bald crown and squints askance at the peculiar trio of strangers occupying the corner booth. "Maybe. They're a long way from Whitehorse Airfield if they are."

Two men and a woman. They were already there when the two officers walked in thirty minutes earlier. Been there a while based on the disarray of their table. They wear office-casual attire—slacks and button shirts under matching blue parkas hanging on the nearby coat tree.

L. Denton blows at a forkful of steaming fries hovering under his chin. "Americans?"

P. Gaboury forks some poutine, then napkins gravy from his lips through a pinch. "If they're American *and* military, they're twice as far from home."

He's watched the trio whispering to one another, often quietly, sometimes in rising, panicked murmurs before one or two of the others tamp it down with gently raised hands and less moderate glares. Occasionally they glimpse out the fogging glass at the eddying snow beyond, as if they're waiting for someone, or dreading that *someone's* very appearance.

L. Denton takes to arranging his silverware perfectly distanced to either side of his plate. What he watched his ex-navy father do at dinner so he wouldn't dwell on the rebukes and censures the old man leveed on his mother for basic existence. "Oil contractors?"

P. Gaboury doesn't reply. Just keeps corner-eyeing the trio and their continuous hushed-but-rattled chatter. Sometimes his eyes roam, invariably landing on the art. The walls are festooned by kitschy paintings and an overkill of Christmas decorations. The kind of hand-me-down fare crafted by family and enduring out of guilt more than actual quality. Tacky if not consistent in color, at least, he thinks. Even the upright piano on the wall between restroom doors has been painted a glossy agave, though for the life of him he can't remember what the bizarre, taxidermied amalgam of rabbit with deer antlers is called that sits atop it.

And then there are the customers. Nearly two dozen in total, most from the bus outside. *Beskin Wildlife Tours* reads the side of the vehicle in what might be a hand-painted script, though what wildlife they were hoping to see in this weather is anyone's guess. The tourists appear mostly retirees. Uncharacteristically loud for their age, but harmless otherwise.

"*Flo-ridians*," L. Denton had muttered to himself the moment he and P. Gaboury strolled into the Last Chance Grill.

"If they're oil," says P. Gaboury, fixing again on the odd trio in the corner, "they're the money half of the operation. Those are *not* the hands of roughnecks."

***

"We're a hundred miles away, Amos," says Doug, wiggling perfectly manicured fingers out the window and adding a daring wink for emphasis. "Whatever those…*things* were, they didn't follow us no hundred miles on foot."

Amos had been right. No sooner had they sat down and got something sloshing through their stomachs did their silent shock transmute at once to avalanched gab. They needed the outlet, however aggravating it was becoming.

"All of which would be moot if the safeguards they fucking hyped up and down creation for a year had been fucking legitimate," Vera says, as if replying to a question from a different conversation. She's ordered the most coffee of the three, already on her fifth cup with a strong leadoff to six.

Doug addresses the space between Vera and Amos. "Whole lot of spilled milk now."

Vera's head snaps at Doug. His tiresome digressions have increased throughout the week, as if he'd sensed the inevitable disaster and had begun sandbagging his own property against the inundation instead of warning others. "Says everyone who could've done something about a catastrophe beforehand, but didn't."

"Distance…might be irrelevant," Amos says, tearing his eyes from the window at last. Even seated, his slender frame still towers over his cohorts. It's an awkwardness he has only recently discovered comfort with at forty. Puberty's reach could tickle stars in other galaxies. He takes a sip from a cup he's steadily refused refilling for an hour.

"Pheromone dissemination topped out at fifty miles…" sing-songs Doug, resting elbows on the booth's backrest.

"Robotic instead of human safeguards, they promised," resumes Vera, still in her third-party conversation. "Machines don't emit pheromones, they said, whatever the fuck that means…"

"I heard one of them yell 'cortisol spiking,' before another rebuked him that a containment breach was inevitable," Amos tells Vera, who stabs back *oh really* eyes. He then regards Doug: "Fifty-mile dissemination was one beta test subject. Hybrid-12 was given a booster last week. The booster *you* designed."

Doug chases a shrug with a smirk. "Touché, Doctor. But I thought we were working with *plants*, not…whatever the hell those things—"

Vera scoffs. "And who, for the love of fuck, designed that Swiss-cheese containment?"

"Not *me*…" Doug mutters.

Amos blinks away the scorn. Vera huffs irritation and bats a dismissive wrist.

A sighing gust outside rattles the glass in its mullions. The groan of swelling wood in old galleons. It reminds Vera of her childhood home—its long, knotted pine floors that creaked like barn door hinges—where her father read her Jules Verne as a way to steer her toward the sciences despite her early aptitude for art that was all but smothered out by the time she reached junior high. She skips wistful eyes over all the art in the diner. Rolling, idyllic landscapes of eerie impression, as if Grant Wood and Grandma Moses sired an impish blend fond of teals and mints. She presumes one of the elderly owners is the artist, and if pressed to wager, would opt for the husband. The tic of a smile wriggles behind her lips, which she stifles by locking on the face echoed in her coffee cup.

"They could've—*should've*—warned us what we were dealing with," she tells the reflection—a most reliable of self-scourges. "I mean, if we were actually in danger of life and limb, which I *didn't* sign up for…"

Amos grumbles either assent or objection under his breath, and his gaze is back out the window tracing snow-laden firs. "We should definitely get down the mountain before dusk. Get to the warmer valley."

Doug slurps the last of his strawberry shake. "As you've said now...*six* times. You know we're not in a climate-controlled lab anymore—"

"Warmer by what?" Vera prompts. "Ten, fifteen degrees tops? If they're governed by your epidermal tests, that'll do fuck-all to slow them down. Jesus, what have we done?"

Doug pokes his straw around his empty glass, coaxing strawberry seeds back to the bottom as if they were ants making a break for it. "Worked on something grander than seed pods and polymer skins, obviously, *Doctor* Ochoa."

Vera grins through her burn. "*Grander* isn't the word you're looking for, *Doctor* Choi. Amos, tell me one more time what you saw."

Amos leans over the table. Though the oldest of the three, his dark, sunken eyes, even in the best of moods, perpetually insinuate the scowl of much older men, and thus work well as silent gavels, a mollifier he learned to appreciate the power of—along with his gangly height—in college with women *and* men. "Those cops at the counter. They keep looking our way."

Doug peers beyond Amos and snorts. "What do you think they suspect? Intellectual supremacy?"

"We're not being as subtle as we think we are," says Amos.

"Understatement of this entire shit-show endeavor," Vera adds, and glances over both shoulders for a server and a refill.

Amos sips from his cold cup, finding the usually over-scorched brew of diner coffee tolerable only after it has cooled down. "The project, Vera, despite the...*faux pas*, is still sound."

A bitter chuckle from Vera, and she holds up her empty cup in a toast. "*Faux pas*..."

The old man who's been minding the kitchen when not serving coffee slaps a dishtowel over his shoulder and grabs a carafe. He ambles over, tall but toil-bent.

"Refill time, refill time," he announces, smiling soft warmth behind a wreath of ashy whiskers. He tops off Vera's cup with a dipped flourish. "Anyone else?"

"None for me, thanks," Amos says.

The old man—Blue, by his name tag—scratches at his beard before shrugging and casting his light-blue eyes toward Doug. "And how about you, young man? Another shake for you?"

Doug grins widely, an expression that wrung additional reprimands from his parents on top of the soiled rugs and scorched furniture his ambitious forays into chemistry had wrought. Despite his older brothers causing the same mayhem before him, he got it the worst of the three, and he wondered if it was because he giggled while generating his chaos. "Oh, my belly can handle but only one shake a day, sir. Wee bit lactose intolerant and all. Say, do you get a lot of law enforcement as regulars here?"

Amos tries vainly to screen a glower behind his cup. Vera is less guarded with her own scowl.

Blue's lips purse, and he wiggles this pucker left-right-left. "Eh, depending on the season. Springs and summers, certainly. Winter, not so much, but it's still *early* winter yet. Too darn early for this kind of snow, I'd say. Especially after the burner of a summer we just had. But at least all those fires are out. Never seen burn like that."

Vera slurps loudly from her cup, letting some dribble down her chin before gripping Blue's wrist in goosed atonement. "So sorry! I…lost myself in the paintings. Are you the artist by chance?"

Blue lights up as if the power had returned after a long blackout. "I so happen to be, yes!"

"Well, I love it all," Vera says, grinning suns—the very expression she stifles in the lab to preserve what respect she can and which she's only now starting to regret, and she feels the scratchy shift in the air as her two colleagues take note of her ruse. "You should be proud, Blue. It's sound work." She catches Amos's eye. "Definitely *very* sound."

"Ah me, well thank you kindly, young lady! And you all flag me down should you change your minds on your drinks."

Once more the old man swells with pride. Crud of some manner has caught in his light-gray whiskers, Vera notices, and seems to actually brighten in the vein of mood stones when he smiles.

Once he's gone, Amos lobs a glower at a self-satisfied Doug before fixing on Vera. "*Sound* was your determination as well regarding the project not forty-eight hours ago."

"I third that conclusion," Doug says. "*Faux pas* notwithstanding."

"Fucking Chernobyl state of mind," Vera whispers. "And way to keep us low-key, *Doctor* Choi. *Say, do you get lots of law enforcement this time of year— look at me playing Ian Fleming spy boy!* Christ…"

Doug leans back into the booth to waft all the self-satisfaction a body can hold—an additional needle that would've earned him a swat as a kid.

She's back on Amos: "Again, *Doctor* Huber, for the cheap seats: What did you see in the lab?"

Amos sucks against his teeth, hoping in vain to shed the inquiry, but Vera's glare practically steams. "Like I said, it moved too fast. All I saw…were eyes."

Vera bites back a snarl. "Okay, eyes. But was it big, small? Did it have, I don't know, a tail, antenna, wings, two fucking heads?"

"Yeah, *Doctor* Huber," Doug says. "Was it like some Area-51 spooky-spooky? Is this what we've been working on all along?"

"You both know as much as I do," Amos says. It barked out more than he'd intended, and he tries to siphon it back through a heavy breath. "What I *barely* saw was small. Maybe half the size of an adult. It was low to the ground. Moved like a cat. Just a blur, really." He whips a quick glance at the cops—especially the nosier bald one—before squinting out the window again. "All right, let's…get the check and keep moving. We need to reach Fort Greely before nightfall. Beat that storm."

***

Officer L. Denton swirls a biscuit around his plate, sponging up as much gravy as it'll hold. "Are they gonna be a problem?"

Officer P. Gaboury keeps his gaze hovering over the corner booth. The taller and older of the strangers has noticed this and keeps snapping eyes back out the window as a result.

"Nah," he says at length, then gestures over the old woman behind the register. "They're too buttoned up."

"Fidgety," L. Denton says. He pops the biscuit into his mouth, chews once, and swallows. "Squirrelly."

The old woman embraces a middle-aged pair of regulars before waving them goodbye. She's still spry for her seventy-or-so years, P. Gaboury notices. Compact but strong. Her stock implies a line of ground-breakers, country-builders. Before starting for the officers, she pauses at the counter and peace-signs the old bearded guy starting a new pot of coffee with a wink. Surely her husband, based on their curt but loving shorthand, but there's no doubt about it: this is *her* place.

"I hope your poutines were as advertised, Officers," she says, a hint of drag in her voice, as if she'd quit cigarettes some time ago, but not before they left their un-scrubbable scorch.

"They certainly were, thank you," P. Gaboury says. "And your place here is…unique."

The woman turns to take it all in as if seeing it herself for the first time. "It is that. The *décor* is compliments of my husband."

P. Gaboury bites back a simper. "It's quite the accumulation."

"With age comes hoarding, but not of things necessarily." she says, stifling her own understatement through a tired sigh. "Should-haves and could-haves make equally impregnable piles."

"Mind if I ask, but are you familiar with the trio at the corner booth?"

The woman—Jill, by her name tag—cocks her eyes their way as if to challenge the fibs of children, and shakes her head. "Can't say I am. Then again, can't say I'm familiar with you two officers either. Then *again*, we're beset by officers and Mounties this time of year. Benefits of having heat *and* coffee. *And* mighty grand poutine. Can I interest you gentlemen in seconds? It's my great aunt's own hush-hush recipe…?"

"No thank you," P. Gaboury says.

As Jill clears their dishes, she lets her gaze settle on each officer for a drawn-out beat. "You suspect them for something illicit? Perhaps they purloined a stapler or two?"

P. Gaboury's face softens enough to cobble a smile from the remnants.

"Oh no. Nothing so grand. Just…don't see many of their matching officious type up these mountains. A curiosity is all. But I will have another Coke, and he'll…?"

He looks at L. Denton who faces his partner and enunciates, "Lon-don Fog," before turning to Jill. "Thank you, no, ma'am. Just water, please."

Jill's glower is the perfect balance of playful suspicion and warning that growls: *Don't you dare break the peace of my place.* "Beverages coming up," she says.

P. Gaboury is surprised by the genuine smile he replies with before chewing it away. He appreciates her working together spunk and skepticism into a respectable balance. He waits for Jill to move off before tilting his head to L. Denton and winking. "Maybe their stocks took a huge dump? Gaudy timeshare they can't get out of? Annoying, but harmless otherwise?"

"Panic's the unfortunate equalizer," L. Denton says.

A flare-up in the kitchen as some lard-drenched sauce swirls off a pan into open flame. The tourists dig into their late lunches, silverware pinging and grating against porcelain, their din a dance of stage-whispered gossip and mouth-stuffed chuckles and guffaws. Their current environment is safe, permissible, liberating. Outside, it's a hundred miles of snowy wood in all direction from what they're likely accustomed to, adding to the freedom from themselves and the stares of others. Lucky them, P. Gaboury thinks.

His attention is roped to the left—to the corner booth—where he catches the tall one stiffening at seeing something out the window, though he himself can't make out anything through the thick fall of snow. Maybe he stumbled upon a way for them all to extricate themselves from whatever situation has them jumpy, he ponders, and now the man is gnawing it over for feasibility before sharing it with his associates.

"I'll handle it if it starts to *equalize*," he says.

L. Denton's brow bobs once. "Duly noted."

***

A glint of light yanks Amos's eyes to the tree line like a choke collar, and all his muscles lock.

There, between crisscrossed pine trunks past the shoulder across the highway—a quick but unmistakable blaze of aquamarine eyes.

"Dammit," he mutters.

Vera latches eyes with his, her own already fear-dilated. "What? Dammit what?"

"They're here."

Doug double-blinks before turning to look out the window. "Wait—are you serious?"

Amos glances at the cops, both of whom are now openly glowering their way. "Serious as a meltdown. Tree line to the east, just past our car."

Vera, up on her knees now, palms to the glass, scans the trees. "Fuck me. How could anything track…?"

"Fifty-mile dissemination limit my ass," Doug says. His expression toggles between delight and terror as he's also on his knees and squinting out the window. Together they evoke children looking out for Santa Claus—if Santa came with fangs and claws and insatiable rage-hunger.

"Shit, shit, shit, shit…" Vera grumbles, shaking her head.

Amos inhales another long breath, letting his hands knuckle crack under the table. Childhood exercises his mother taught him to combat anxiety. The throb in his lower leg has only slightly abated, but flares up whenever he shifts it—which has been a lot since they'd arrived. "Okay, okay. We need…to barricade the place. Gather everyone in the center. Climate control…"

"Barricade?" Doug prompts through a snort. "It's one goddamn spooky whatever thing out there. And climate control what? This a Podunk diner, not a state-of-the-art research facility."

Vera, brow knotted, mouths a tumble of vague words, as if wading through some calculus that won't jibe. "Last verified count was eighteen in that containment batch—all freshly re-enhanced. Except we thought they were *plants*. No, no—we need to get everyone out *right* now and make a break while we—"

Four elk crash through the trees then and sprint in single file down the highway, including a marvelous 14-point bull who bugles warning or panic. Several diners *ooh* and *ahh* at the spectacle, some frantically trying in vain to locate their phone cameras while a couple voice their wish for a rifle.

"Too late," Doug says, all his sarcasm wilting in real time. "Wait—where're you going?"

But Amos is already up. Up and marching with a hitch in his step toward the police officers at the counter.

***

L. Denton sets down his glass of water perfectly within the center of a Moosehead Lager coaster and says, "Equalization appears underway."

P. Gaboury runs a sleeve across dry lips and slips off his stool. "And I'm on it."

***

Despite mostly tourists in the room, Amos nonetheless feels the burr of their eyes as he approaches the officers. As if they know he and his table are the incongruity there, even more than themselves. The anomaly that doesn't match the others. It's an unease he's used to; the conveyance of some other role or occupation—politician, attorney, company chairman. *Anything* but a researcher and engineer. And certainly not a police officer, like his father was and wanted his only boy to be, and the brief lament has him gliding a hand along the cushioned edge of the counter to keep straight and moving.

His leg burns more than ever. Vera had noticed him favoring it when he used the bathroom as soon they arrived at the diner, and inquired about it right when he got back. He'd told her it was from a fall during the sudden chaos of the lab breach not five hours earlier. She merely replied with a pressed-lipped nod.

Doug, bless his heart, remained completely oblivious.

"Officers, may I have a word?" says Amos as soon as he's within earshot. Immediately the shorter bald officer hops off his stool and slips a hand into his open shearling bomber, and Amos's hands rise to either side. "Easy, Officer. My name is Dr. Amos Huber, and if I may, we have a problem. A potentially very serious problem."

P. Gaboury's hand emerges from the jacket holding an automatic, which he promptly levels between Amos's eyes.

The diners gasp in unison, with a couple yelping as if centipedes had just skittered over their bare toes in the shower.

"Oh yeah," P. Gaboury says. "You all most certainly have a *very* serious problem, *Doc.*"

3

AS QUICKLY AS panic swelled the room, a brief lull of silence ensues, as if from the shocked aftermath of a fender bender, or an upended bottle of wine over a white rug.

P. Gaboury's gun, inches from Amos's forehead, holds as level and steady as stone. "Ladies and gentlemen, kindly remain seated, kindly remain calm," he announces with a startling-to-him authority that coincidentally serves verisimilitude on a plate. "Is the Beskin present of Beskin Wildlife Tours?"

A shared murmur slips from the patrons, as if they, too, needed that heavy silence to just die, and at length a middle-aged ginger with a patchy goatee and long ponytail rises on wobbly legs. "Uh…yes, sir, Officer?"

"That your bus outside?" P. Gaboury asks.

A swallow further distends Beskin's already prodigious Adam's apple. "That's correct, sir, yes. My daddy's business, but mine now." Though his mouth is empty, he speaks as if chewing through a mouthful of Red Vines.

"What I'd like for you to do, Mr. Beskin, is to quickly but orderly, get your customers back on the bus." He glances back at L. Denton, who has one hand over his holster while the other cups the shoulder CB radio he's mouthing into. "If everyone will please follow Mr. Beskin to the bus. As you can see, we do have a situation, but it is well under control, and we're calling in backup as I speak, so don't you fret yourselves. And don't worry about your bills. Today's meal will be compliments of the Royal Canadian Mounted Police."

Despite the general anxiety and confused grumblings of the rising diners, a few whistles and whoops in salute of a free lunch crest the din. Beskin, with only one arm in his parka, is already out the door and jogging to the bus. The more ambulatory of the diners are right behind him.

"Officer, please," Amos whispers. "Don't send people out there. We need to fortify in here."

P. Gaboury's arm extends forward, sliding his weapon's muzzle two inches closer to the interloper's forehead.

Amos swallows and edges forward until the gun's sight dents the skin of his forehead.

P. Gaboury's head tilts from surprise and curiosity. The man is either death-wishing, or as serious as bowel cancer.

"You don't understand," Amos continues—less a whisper now and more of a growl. "You need to get these people back inside. There's something dangerous out there—*lethal*—and you're putting them all at risk."

"Oh yeah?" P. Gaboury says, loud enough for everyone to hear. "I'd say there's something dangerous in *here*."

That puts the pep into the steps of some of the stragglers, and soon they're all outside in a haphazard line to the open bus doors, stomping against the fresh cold.

Amos, having backed away from the gun, glances at their booth. Both Vera and Doug are still on their knees, alternately gawking at their partner while searching the tree line, hands white-knuckling the orange backrest. They see it just as Amos does: the same glimpse of greenish-blue eyes between the trees stirring the bracken to the west. He's about to appeal to P. Gaboury again when he notices that his gun has drifted slightly into the dining room.

"You two," P. Gaboury snaps at a pair of diners at a different window booth. Two men in their late twenties, freshly exploded off an L.L Bean catalogue. "Kindly get onto the bus. Heck, I don't care if it's kindly at this point, just get the fuck on."

"We're...not with that tour," one of them says, a jowly blond with a man bun.

"We're on a hiking trip," pipes up his buddy across from him in a too-stylish-to-be-local Eddie Bauer ushanka.

P. Gaboury looks out the window. Most of the blue-hairs are aboard the bus. He looks over at L. Denton and says, "Block it," before addressing the two hikers again. "I'm assuming yours is that glossy silver Humvee taking up two spaces?"

Both the hikers look out wide-eyed as if to verify their ride is still there and indeed occupying more than one space. They nod concurrently at the officer.

The gun drifts back to Amos.

"And I assume the Toyota RAV4 tucked on the opposite shoulder is yours and your posse's?"

Arms akimbo, Amos nods, a small Rorschach of sweat itching through his button-up at mid-chest.

P. Gaboury winks. "Smart not to park it in the lot. Easier getaway, right? In case of panic, or a stalled engine from the cold bottlenecking everyone in?"

Amos shakes his head. The ridiculousness of the situation couldn't be more farcical if thought bubbles had begun sprouting above everyone's head. "Please, Officer. At least…turn up the heat in here. As high as it'll go."

The resultant frown causes P. Gaboury's gun to dip slightly. Whatever the odd trio's reason for being here—aside from the opportunistic distraction they've provided—he can't yet figure out, but he hadn't expected it to be this abnormal.

Something lethal out in the woods?

Turn up the diner's heat?

Up comes the gun again. "Shut up, Doc," he snarls, and his eyes bank out the window at the bus again.

No sooner is the last passenger aboard and the doors shut than the idling bus revs once, then starts crunching over the snow banked along the shoulder before wobbling back onto the highway.

As it clears the lot, L. Denton drags out of their police pickup a stack of sawhorses that he proceeds to line side by side until they block the road.

Amos blows out a held breath. Those tourists were old and slow, which means they might have some time yet. The one set of eyes he saw out there is likely just an advance scout who won't risk a solo attack.

"Everybody else!" P. Gaboury says. "That means you two weekend Lewis and Clarks, as well as all employees in and out of the kitchen: your turn to kindly skedaddle." He nods his gun once at Amos, then twice beyond him at Vera and Doug. "You three oddballs get to stay."

Up to then, the elderly owners, Blue and Jill, had taken a position by the register, quietly urging the customers out. Once vacated, they remained side by side, hands clasped. Now Jill breaks their hold and gestures the two cooks out of the kitchen and urges them along, telling them to take the rest of the day off. At the same time, the two weekend hikers rise and gobble down the last of their burgers and gulp the last of their pops before filing out.

"Thank you, gentlemen, thank you for your cooperation," P. Gaboury says. "And I'm sure you'll be able to skirt around those barricades on your way out without touching them." When he looks back to the register, he sees that Jill has resumed her place beside Blue in their own Canuck version of *American Gothic*. "Uh, you too, mom and pop. This is a police matter, so kindly vacate, or you might not beat that storm. Be just awful if you found yourselves stranded on these roads."

Jill steps forward until she's almost abreast of Amos, ire and worry dueling in her eyes.

"We're not leaving. This is our place, and my husband and I assume the risk—*Officers*, or…whatever."

P. Gaboury suckles away on a tart smile, his instincts about her being spot on. "Well now, that's quite the mistake."

L. Denton reenters the diner, lugging with him a large duffle bag and a police scanner under his thick arm. He places them on the counter, unzips the bag, and draws out a scoped hunting rifle from it.

"We know all the police officers for fifty miles around, and we've never seen you pair before," Jill says, arms crossed.

Behind her, Blue raises a hand to mitigate before dropping it back down, surely used to the futility of trying to corral his wife's bluntness.

P. Gaboury dips his gun once at her before retraining it on Amos. "One point for you, Jill. Except now you're gonna get to know us *really* well. See, Smiles and I were content enough holding onto these three outsiders as hostages, but five works out fine too. And if you're cooperative, everyone here will sleep safe and sound in their own beds tonight."

Amos watches L. Denton—of late, *Smiles*—take to his tasks with the rote efficiency of someone honed under crop of short time constraints between observations. A man accustomed to counting guard steps and shift changes in his sleep. For his size and bulk, he moves fast. No—*efficiently*, Amos checks himself. Not a single effort wasted in checking weapons for load. The same for the other, P. Gaboury, and as if a spotlight of different hue and color temperature had been splashed upon them, Amos now sees these two men in police dress entirely differently just by how they hold their eyes. These aren't purloined stares augmented by proximity to a fraternity of like-minded bullies bolstered by legal permissibility and pensions, but rather the eyes of men who would shatter your teeth for no other reason than they're in your mouth and they don't like the look of them.

"If you're here to rob us," says Jill, unable to beat down the swallow that follows the declaration, "you're going to be disappointed."

P. Gaboury lets his concrete glare press on Jill before softening it with a slashed grin. "I see no reason to doubt that. But we're definitely not here for money."

"Then what do you want?" Amos prompts. The terseness of voice surprised him most of all, though P. Gaboury isn't far behind with his arched brow, grin, and jiggling of gun at Amos as if drawing everyone's attention to the dog doing funny tricks on the rug.

"Get these bookworms?" he says, glancing back at his partner who's only paying heed to the tasks within a few feet of his eyes. P. Gaboury studies his watch a moment, using his gun's sight to scratch the side of his temple. "Well, I was going to wait a bit to share our plan, but what the hell? In about ninety minutes' time, a prison bus will be passing by. Since this is the last stop for food and bathrooms for the next sixty miles of winding mountain road—plus one roadblock—they will be stopping. Inside of said bus sits one of our colleagues, and before their pitstop is complete, said colleague, Smiles, and myself will be leaving separately—"

A loud crash and clatter, and they all turn to see that L. Denton has brought the butt of his rifle down on the wall phone near the bathrooms before proceeding to the phone by the register and ripping it out of its jack.

"Thank you, Smiles, for the reminder," P. Gaboury says. "Everyone, kindly relinquish all cellular phones to my colleague."

Smiles moves to the booth, a thick, workman's hand extended. Both Vera and Doug gawk at Amos, who just nods back. They fish out their phones and hand them over to Smiles, who then proceeds to Blue, who just shrugs.

"My husband...has never been fond of cell phones," Jill says.

Smiles nonetheless frisks him, and upon finding nothing, moves up to Jill and Amos and takes their already extended phones.

"Now then," P. Gaboury says, "best thing we all can do now—"

But the shrill screaming from outside cuts him off like a thunderclap.

***

Everything beyond the windows reads as overlapped film strips at first—so much running, struggling, and puzzling separation of parts from bodies.

But the blood is crystal-clear, exploding against the snow like projector beams.

The first distinct image they will all remember later in a relative moment of calm is the jowly hiker trying to hop back to the diner on one leg while the other drags behind by a few strands of flesh below the knee, his mouth a blasted "O" of shock and confusion.

"Lock the door!" Amos yells.

The only other not moored to a booth or the floor—L. Denton, aka Smiles—bounds to the door and slaps home the upper and lower bolts. He unshoulders his rifle but holds it at a forty-five, the shock of it all still setting stakes in him as well.

Because he sees them now. They *all* see them now.

Sleek, sinuous forms on all fours, eyes blazing white-hot cobalt in the vein of cats when the right incidental light angle catches their retinas. Though they move too quickly for a clearer look, it's enough to tell that their hides are hairless, ranging from gray to muted blues. Except for the degree of blood smeared about them.

Two pounce suddenly from either side and take down the jowly hiker, one plunging teeth into his neck and sending arterial flow in arcs against the diner's windows, while the other finishes the leg amputation with one swipe of a taloned paw.

To the left of the lot, one of the cooks—a young, mustachioed Gwich'in—plays a weak, fading tug-of-war with one of the creatures, using his own entrails as a rope, while the other cook—an older metalhead in a Slayer shirt—drags himself screaming in vain toward his car with his one remaining arm, while two of the creatures furiously thrash to wishbone his legs apart at the hips.

At their grisly wrenching loose, Jill and Blue utter matching yelps they quickly muffle with a hand before blanketing each other in a *don't look* embrace.

The diner windows on the right are suddenly pelted with a fan of snow, and everyone reflexively ducks through their shock as the silver Humvee, swarmed by four of the creatures on the outside, peels in a half-donut before gunning straight through the parking lot and across the road, only to T-bone directly into the RAV4 on the opposite shoulder. The impact accordions the Toyota, sending it teetering and finally rolling down the embankment.

A fascinated yet disheartened *Fuck* seeps from Doug at seeing the last of their vehicle tumble out of sight.

Just as the Humvee corner-clips the trunk of an aspen, the other hiker dives out of the driver's seat and rolls on the snow. He rises in an artless flail of limbs, ushanka ear flaps spun about his head, and manages about a dozen feet of slippery, aimless run before he's set upon by three of the creatures.

Smiles, having gathered himself, draws the bolt on his rifle to verify a round, and starts to unlock the front door, but Amos quickly bearhugs him from behind.

"No! It's too late!"

With little effort, Smiles shrugs the rangy man off, but remains by the door, sucking back equine breaths as he watches the hiker plead and shriek as the beasts essentially draw-and-quarter him to pieces.

"Jill. *Jill!*" Amos barks. Gradually her head creaks his way, her fully dilated eyes wicking tears. "Turn up the heat. As high as you can get it—right now!"

Her head shakes an initial *no*, but it's only a reflex—her body breaking its paralysis. Blue's hand finds hers again and squeezes, and she turns and palms his cheek. She mutters something to him, and he starts for the back. "He's doing it," she tells Amos.

"What…the fuck are those things?" P. Gaboury mutters. Throughout the attack he'd kept his gun raised in the general direction of Amos, but shock has rendered his grip otherwise numb and adrift. His eyes slowly track to his own hand, and he finally lowers his weapon through a shudder.

"Lock the back door while you're there!" Vera, the next to thaw out, calls in Blue's direction.

That seems to defrost everyone else as well. Doug, mouth trembling, slowly shimmies out of the booth and side-steps toward Amos, his eyes tethered out the window.

Smiles retreats to the counter and starts drawing more guns from his satchel—several pistols and a twelve-gauge pump-action.

"What the bunny-fuck are those things?" P. Gaboury prompts, this time clearly and with a hatchet's edge.

Doug, being in his direct line of sight in the moment, hitches his shoulder in a child's shrug.

"Heat's turned up and the back door's locked as well as the storeroom roll-up," Blue says, as if stating the day's lunch special. Jill shoots him a look as if he were a child goofing off during church service, and Blue totters quietly over, fidgeting with his beard.

"We don't know," Vera says. She'd wandered to the coffee station and was helping herself too casually to another cup. The carafe's mouth rattles against the cup like bashing typewriter hammers. "But temperature extremes…might hold them at bay." And her eyes search out and bury into Amos's like spades into dirt.

P. Gaboury's gun rises again at no one in particular, but just as quickly drops back down to his side. "And how the hell do you know that?"

Amos, who's been leaning against the bar, arms crossed and head down to better let his mind run all manner of survival scenario permutations, looks up and fixes matter-of-factly on P. Gaboury. "Because we might've made them."

Smiles, who'd sidled up to his partner by then, is about to pose his own question when Jill gasps and points to the front door.

Standing against the glass, albeit on two legs now, is one of the creatures. Only then does their initial disconcerting nature start to clarify to everyone in the diner.

The creatures are at least partially human. And they're no more than children.

***

Whatever of them that is still human is undeniable, however uncanny: the blemishless facial features above the nose, the narrow, slim build and shorter stature.

Everything else, however, defies such a moniker, and as the dining room gawks at this panting, blood-stippled specimen taking them all in from behind the glass of the front door, they all register different incongruities at the same time—a reenactment of the parable of the blind men and the elephant: grayish skin near porcelain in texture, the reverse-hinged knee joint scarred and pustuled in breaching mechanical micro-components, the serrated claw tips at the ends of extended fingers trickling blood on the snow by equally distended and taloned toes, the slight feline muzzle protrusion at the mouth behind which breach inch-long canines, eyes gleaming like computer screens in dark rooms.

Its right hand rises then and palms the door. Elongated fingers that appear equipped with an extra joint curl and wind against the glass as if playing some exotic instrument.

Smiles shoulders his rifle, but Amos quickly steps in and upends the barrel, sending an inadvertent round into the acoustical ceiling panels.

General yelps from the unexpected and deafening discharge, and Smiles bolts out the spent round and jacks in a fresh load before training his rifle on Amos's chest.

"That glass," Amos stutters, swallows, then musters his carriage ramrod straight. "The temperature difference between inside and out—it's the only thing keeping us alive."

Smiles, eyes narrowed and blistering, only slightly lowers his weapon.

All eyes turn in unison back to the creature, still standing at the door, thoroughly unreactive to the gunshot. They watch as it yanks back its hand suddenly from the glass, as if a flame from a lighter had been clicked under it. It blows uncertainty through its mouth, launching spittle into the glass before it turns and bounds off with a gazelle's speed and grace back toward the tree line.

The rest of the creatures emerge from behind vehicles, cagey and deferential, whereupon they gather up whatever pieces of the dead they can carry before following what is surely their leader back into the trees, leaving patches of red-black gore the increasing snowfall is promptly dusting over.

"The hell…are they doing?" P. Gaboury whispers.

"They're scatter-hoarding," Doug says, his voice, though low, almost erupting in the space by dint of its sobriety.

Another voice—Smiles'—performs the same disruption through its own diffident and basso nature: "Those aren't chipmunks and crows. Never seen predators hoard."

"My guess is they've been adapted for it," Doug says, the awe in his tone suggesting it more revelation than knowledge, and a revived confidence allows him to edge himself between Smiles and Amos. "They've…likely already found some tree hollow or cave in which to stash the meat."

"The *meat?*" Jill says, and all in the room are instantly drawn to the grief shuddering her eyes as they linger about the puddles outside that mark the last of what remains of her massacred co-workers and friends.

"Sorry," Doug mutters, his skin chilling to goosebumps despite the fast-rising temperature of the diner.

"They're weakest during an adaptation cycle," Amos says, drawing eyes to himself to spare Doug becoming *that* person on which to dump collective fault, umbrage, and ultimately mob-punishment. "It's why I had the heat turned up, otherwise they might've barreled right through the glass. Now that their alpha knows there's an extreme temperature difference between us and the outside, they won't risk an assault. They'll likely just wait us out. See which of us is crazy enough to make a run for it."

"What's to stop them from hurling rocks?" says Smiles, nee L. Denton. He's back at the counter starting up the police scanner he'd brought in from their truck. "Shatter the glass, let the temperature balance out, walk right in and tear us apart?"

Amos frowns his thoughts, and at length points at Smiles' shouldered rifle. "Our *fortuitous* discharge. Despite their more animalistic instincts having been amplified, we shouldn't assume that they're stupid. They understand we're armed and a threat. We got lucky."

"But they're just...kids," P. Gaboury says, only to double-blink and stiffen his stance at relinquishing to the room so vulnerable a moment.

"Radically augmented kids," Amos says. "Judging by their speed and strength, you'd essentially be scrapping with a mountain lion, not a child. I recommend we try remaining as calm as possible."

"Hooch," mutters a voice. Only Doug hears it as coming from Smiles.

"The storm might give us an added advantage," Vera says, stepping in to join the loose huddle. Despite the nearly eighty-degrees-and-climbing temperature inside, she double-grips her coffee mug as if to warm her hands. "That, and dusk will create a wider safety buffer, so..."

Again from Smiles, only now hissed: "*Hooch.*"

P. Gaboury shakes his head. "Well, we won't be staying that long—"

"Hooch!" Smiles barks this time, slamming a hand on the countertop and bouncing the police scanner an inch off the surface, putting the flinch in Doug loitering nearest to him.

P. Gaboury turns to protest, but stops dead at seeing his partner's pressed, quivering-lipped glare. "What? *What*, for god's sake?"

"The prison bus," Smiles says. "They're waiting out the storm before coming up the mountain. Best estimate is dawn at the earliest before they reach us."

P. Gaboury's—*Hooch's*—shoulders wilt. The shrinkage is hardly noticeable, even if any of the others had been looking at him instead of at Smiles in the moment, but he self-admonishes nonetheless at once more betraying weakness. A trait cited more than once, albeit fondly, by House— Smiles' brother, and the man they're here to break free.

Except that now they'll be waiting till morning at the earliest for that chance.

Hooch turns to Amos and nods his gun at him.

"Start talking. What are we dealing with? What the fuck did you lunatics make?"

4

AMOS SIDLES TO a counter stool in fatigued strides, hoping that alone might camouflage his limp, though it likely divulges it even more so. He swivels to face the room and crosses arms—not locked and terse, but hands cupping elbows in the stress-free manner one might employ to cradle an infant for a long spell. "Truthfully, we're not sure what those things are. Not...fully. We're part of what's called, informally, the Miami Project. Some intern's joke about Miami having optimum weather year-round, never mind that for a sizeable portion of the population, humidity isn't their friend. In any case, it's a study on how to make plants better adapt physiologically to drastic changes in climate. That"—he flaps a hand toward the outside—"was what broke containment in our lab early this morning instead of...*plants*."

"What lab?" prompts Hooch.

"Fort Selkirk," Doug says, and immediately glances apologetically at Amos who's folded up again into strategy mode.

"But that's...an old trading post," Jill says. "For tourists."

Doug nods. "*Above* ground, yes."

Hooch's muddled eyes roam about before screeching to a halt again on Amos.

"You said you *might've* made them. The hell did you mean by that?"

Amos glances at his colleagues. Registers Doug's almost innocent, burgeoning realization of his complicity, along with Vera's dreadful resignation to her own. Despite her more macro, peripheral role than Doug's more focused one, she was always the more level-headed. The more versatile, and thus, the most adaptable. Something he would never dare tell Doug. "It means a group of scientists and engineers were brought together over the course of a year under one pretense, then had all our disparate efforts exploited for some other goal, unbeknownst to us."

A loud jostling of furniture upends everyone's thoughts, and all eyes just catch Vera righting a bar stool she failed to summit. She opts for a lower chair at a table she first points at vacantly before pressing hands to her sides as if fighting off runner's cramps.

"You know an awful lot about their tactics for someone claiming the government pulled the wool over your eyes," says Hooch.

Amos watches Vera take a seat at last and bury her head between folded arms on the tabletop before resuming.

"My expertise is in synthetic-to-organic polymers. I was assigned to fabricate a skin that can adapt to and survive large temperature swings. The quick glimpse I got of…one of them…before we escaped, I recognized the textural quality of their hides. They've been encased with my work. It's my reasoning for raising the heat in here. The plants would…the *creatures* would be at their weakest and most vulnerable while readapting to the wide temperature shift. That's what the one at the door was doing. Gauging advantage versus disadvantage."

Hooch lets his scowl simmer over Amos before shifting it to Doug.

"And you? How do you know about scatter-hoarding? Pardon me if you don't strike me as an experienced hunter."

Doug mulls over the question through a sheepish grin. "Doug Choi. *Doctor* Doug Choi. I'm a geneticist. And as it so happens, my primary focus *is* on predators, specifically in their adaptability to encroaching human environments. I was brought into… I was *told* that I was hired onto the project because my dissertation was on African canines and felines acclimating their diets to better digest vegetation and human garbage due to dwindling hunting grounds. Mutations in digestive enzymes, and so forth. Joke's on me, I guess."

"Oh yeah," Hooch says without a shred of irony. He nods at Vera, whose head is still nestled between the shelter of her arms. "And your excuse?"

"Vera's an environmental scientist," Amos says. "While Dr. Ochoa's doctorate is in sociology, she was brought in to—"

"To serve them their test subjects on a silver platter," Vera's muffled voice pipes through her twined arms before her head rises, creaking up as if winched through rusting gears. Her eyes are red, puffy, distant. Her lips are frozen in a pout, as if she'd been cut off in mid-sentence and is just waiting for her interrupter to stop talking so she can resume. "For the last two years, I've studied orphans, cast-offs, abandoned children in Russia and Asia. Specifically, those surviving in the streets or even the wild. More specifically, those in hospitals in terminal conditions of malnutrition or cancer because of surviving without said reliable housing and food. Once hired onto the project, all my intellectual property became theirs. Not just my studies on how they survived on coarse vegetation, but names and locations too. Names of dying kids. Not plants. Dying *kids*, who will now turn us into dying adults."

She pops *Happy now?* eyes at Hooch before reburying her head between her arms.

"Fucking eggheads," Hooch snarls, turning away in disgust.

"What happens now?" Smiles asks, hands spread on the counter, shoulders hunched high in simian menace. Everything about his carriage suggests he'd rather let physique speak than his mouth.

"Right now, they're likely stashing their…*plunder*," Doug says, averting his eyes from Jill and Blue. "Then they'll regroup and, if they still possess rudimentary intelligence of human children between eight and fifteen, plan their next move."

"*Plan?*" echoes Hooch. It tumbles out through a laugh.

"Yes, and quicker than we'd like," Amos says, rising from his stool. He starts pacing in tight, five-foot increments. Though he stands a reedy six-four, he still carries himself high when he walks, as if at the end of a cable just starting to lift him off the floor. His tight, corded neck suggests an aggressiveness to his bearing, as if he wasn't always tall, and he can't let go of his contempt over a growth spurt's leisurely tardiness. "At dawn, they'll be at their weakest as their systems reacclimate to sun warmth, such as it'll be. In this moment, right now, they're perfectly primed for the cold. Perfectly primed to make whatever attack they may or may not do. If I may suggest, we should consider defensive tactics throughout the night—watch duty, and the like—and inventory weapons."

"Oh yeah," Hooch chuckles. "Weapons for *everybody*, sure, Doc."

"I've got a shotgun in the back," Blue says.

Jill merely closes her eyes and squeezes his hand.

Hooch fires back a wide grin. "Do you now?" He turns to Smiles and cocks his head toward Blue.

Smiles groans, hitches his rifle, and starts for Blue, stabbing an adamant finger to the back for the old man to lead the way.

For the first time since his initial approach to what he thought were police officers, Amos squares up to Hooch again. "You think this is the right time to let paranoia be your guide? You see what we're up against out there."

"I'm going to go out on a limb and guess that you and your clever cohorts are absent military training of any kind?" And to further convey his utter lack of intimidation of Doctor Huber—or any other PhD in the room—Hooch leans against the counter and plucks several napkins from a dispenser to wipe his crown of sweat before leisurely shucking off his coat.

"That's presumptuous, not to mention irrelevant," Amos says, swapping hardboiled eyes with Hooch. He's dealt with the type before. The arrogance, the banal, superficial suppositions. Dealt with it his whole life like some did disease or handicap, except his was called *Father*. "You're not dealing with military tactics out there, but animalistic ones."

"I've fired a few nine-mils in my day," Doug offers. He might as well have sharted his skivvies for all it served him.

"Point still holds, Doc. If you're neither proficient nor comfortable with firearms, especially during highly stressed situations, you're as dangerous as those things out there. That said, no one else touches a gun but me and Smiles, clear?"

Blue reenters the room then, followed by Smiles cradling a stacked-bore twelve-gauge.

"Searched the office," he says. "In case they've got a side-piece stashed. Nothing."

Hooch nods. "All right then. Per Doctor Huber's *concern*, Smiles and I will set up watch shifts. Jill and Blue, if you please, some pre-dinner coffee will not go amiss."

Jill turns to Blue, who's already on it—content to engage in a familiar task not under the glare of armed men. She unwinds her scarf darned by Blue last year for their silver anniversary, folds it, and deposits it carefully in a drawer under the register. She starts for Hooch, passing a perturbed Amos who doesn't meet her eyes, and who plunks himself down at the table across from Vera, who might or might not be asleep, but whose mind roils through its own personal tempest either way.

Rolling up his sleeves, Hooch considers Jill's approach with the same nonchalance he employed with the doctor. "If you're hoping for an apology for our intrusion into your business, ma'am, you can heel-toe it back that way. That said, our sincere intent is to not hurt anybody, at least those not directly connected with the ones detaining our colleague."

"You can *kindly* shove your apology," Jill says, her gaze iron-hot. "What I would like to know, *Hooch*, is what you and *Smiles* over there have done with officers L. Denton and P. Gaboury. I'm guessing you didn't just find those name tags at the local Halloween store."

Hooch finds himself torn between meeting her glower or grinning against it. Either would be insulting, so he settles on cool and detached. "Well, they're alive, I can assure you of that. What we drugged them with won't wear off for twenty-four hours at least. They'll wake up nauseous and confused, and with headaches that'll make them wish they still had their guns to blow their brains out with, but otherwise none the worse for wear."

Jill's glare keeps heat-wavering. "And I'm supposed to believe that?"

Hooch shrugs. His fingers piano-tinkle over his gun while his mouth pinches away sour musings. "Believe it. Or don't. But neither Smiles nor myself has ever killed outside a battlefield. We find our aptitudes better suited toward high-end burglary and theft. Give us a good heist over spilling unnecessary blood. Murder is unprofessional. Murder is for amateurs, jilted lovers, and rich politicians."

Blue approaches the bar and places a cup and saucer by Hooch with cured-in affability. Just as Hooch reaches for the cup, Jill takes it, slurps loudly, and walks away with the coffee. There's no stopping Hooch's wide-flaring grin and avalanching, usually guarded charisma.

Outside, the snowfall has increased, and already the light wanes toward a rapidly looming dusk. On the parking lot, whatever evidence of the carnage not half-an-hour old has mostly been smothered to near-virgin purity.

He turns in time to see Jill dump his intended coffee into a floor sink under the kitchen pass-through before settling into a stool behind the register. In the kitchen itself, Blue is affixing an apron, no doubt set on starting dinner to keep his mind busy and distracted. Over at one table, the woman scientist Vera is still playing ostrich, while Amos sits across her in a self-straitjacket staring out the window. To his left, Smiles is checking each weapon for safety and readiness, keeping his rifle slung and holstering a SIG Sauer before dragging a chair a pair of yards shy of the door and settling into it.

The younger scientist, Doug Choi, sits himself at a table equidistant between his associates and Smiles.

Not at all how he'd envisioned or planned it, ponders Hooch—a motley crew of hostages, a delayed bus, a mounting storm, and a pack of man-eating child-monsters lurking in the trees—but what was life but improvising against obstacles, manmade or otherwise? One of House's most oft-muttered quotes, usually following a snort, usually while glaring at a particularly testy and tyrannical guard he imagined shivving through the liver.

"All right then, ladies and gentlemen," he says. "Get cozy. Smiles will take the first watch. But should any of you see shiny eyes out there, don't be shy and speak up. Like it or not, we're in this together till sunup at least."

***

The transition between dusk and full dark is sudden, lost in prolonged eye-pinches and elephantine sighs, and the silence allows for the howl of mounting wind and the cat-canter pelting of snow against glass.

Doug, who's been sitting by himself, knees bouncing like mistimed engine pistons, at last slips off his chair and laps his table a few times in a bored, wide-legged lope before wandering where Smiles is perched by the front door.

"Hope it's okay if I hang out here for a bit? I'm much more Zen if I can see them coming."

Smiles rolls a curt, assessing glance that equates to a *whatever* shrug.

He's never known someone who's done time, and now Doug understands what that hard look he's always heard about means. He gulps back all that the glare implies, and says, "African wild dog."

A muscle seemingly as large as anything on Doug's arm twitches in Smiles' neck. Whether another prison-acquired mannerism or peaked curiosity, Doug has poked his attention-centers at least.

"Hyena?" Smiles says.

Doug's head performs a jaunty yes-and-no head-bounce, and he's immediately thankful that Smiles isn't looking his way to see it. "No. As in they're a different species. Hyena are actually more closely related to cats and mongoose than dogs, if you can believe that." He follows it with a chuckle that splats against Smiles like a gnat on a windshield. "Part of my experiment was testing the feasibility of splicing elements of hyena DNA into the diurnal nature of African wild dogs. Diurnal meaning they hunt during the day—"

"I know what *diurnal* means," Smiles says. Patience seeps from his eyes like smoke.

"Okay... So I was saying, the idea was to splice the hyena's kleptoparasitic nature..."

He glances at Smiles, who finally glances back.

"Food thieves."

Doug stifles a nod, turning him momentarily into a bobblehead. He considers pointing out Smiles' tonal similarity to Johnny Cash, but shoots down fast that surely recurrent comparison. "Taking the food thief element of the hyena and integrating it with the daytime hunting of the African wild dog, along with the nocturnal hunting instinct in cats. All to maximize survival abilities, etcetera, etcetera."

The words drift feather-like to the checkered linoleum. The ever-present bombing comedian squatting in Doug flushes a frigid overflow of nerves down his legs and he alternately shuffles back his feet in the manner of dogs kicking away grass after a long-deferred shit.

"My brother," Smiles says, "always had pipedreams of big game hunting in Africa. Too damned expensive, though, for the common man."

So surprised by the response is Doug that he has to replay the scene again in his mind, this time with subtitles on.

"Your brother...live around these parts?"

A humorless snort tumbles from Smiles—surely the equivalent of a quality guffaw from any other man. "Currently he resides in a prison bus."

Unlike Smiles, Doug can't help the expressions his face vomits forth; in this case, guileless wonder at the scheme of it all. "You mean the guy you're busting out is your actual brother?"

Another prolonged beat sucks the air from the room, suggesting no response in the offing, but enough oil has been spritzed on the hinges to allow for more egress. "House is indeed my blood brother, yes. Surrogate...older brother to Hooch." He huffs like a horse grunting against a stable invader. He checks his rifle, but it's a mechanical effort, either from boredom, chagrin, or frustration. "Job in Whitehorse went bad. Bank job. Round this time two years ago. House took a round in the neck. We thought him dead. Hooch did, at any rate. We... *I* should've gone back for him regardless. Not a soldier's way, leaving a comrade behind."

For the rare times in his life, Doug is rendered speechless. And he hates it. It's nudity-on-Fifth-Avenue levels of awkwardness. He mulls over some appropriate reply, something to *bond* over—perhaps the contentiousness he felt toward his own brothers—but the morsels are small and smack bland in the mouth. Words to be tangled on self-meshed netting. He looks down at his hands, soft and in constant flex against carpal tunnel, and until this moment, he's never drawn back the sheet on his advantages and good fortune. His dearth of adversity. Having seen slaughter now firsthand over the past twelve hours, it shudders him to the core to have been so untouched and non-scarred, and his ensuing swallow feels like he's trying to slug back his own liquified corpse in one chug.

"You think…it's a failure in life, Smiles, if one has never…"

Smiles rises abruptly, and with one arm easily sweeps Doug back a few steps from the door.

"We have eyes," he says.

Juddering from the morass of his thoughts, Doug sees them now too, blinking irregularly through the slicing snow from the tree line like collision lights through a foggy skyline, and he echoes Smiles: "Heads up, everyone—we got eyes!"

Hooch swivels forward in his stool and un-safeties his gun. Others stir wherever they're perched, or huddle tighter within themselves at the specks of eyes, cued on at once as if to illuminate a performance.

Amos rises and moves to Jill and Blue.

"We should turn off the lights. The parking lot halogens are enough to see them coming. Let's not make it easier for them to see us in here."

Blue moves to do so, and in segments, the dining room lights shut off.

Outside, like UFOs in a night sky, some of the eyes shift away to either side. Some even rise, likely taking to the trees for a better bearing. For several minutes this light spectacle continues, a coordinated movement in various directions, all controlled and very clearly synchronized, but none breach through the tree line.

Doug, no longer holding to his seeing-them-coming edict of a few minutes ago, sidles back to the table and joins Vera, who appears more alert and present.

"Fucking creepy-ass blinkers," he says. "How are you doing?"

Vera stares out the window while wiping the crud from the corners of her eyes. "Tired. A bit barfy at…*that*. To which you can obviously add scared-shitless. How are you?"

He thumbs at Smiles. "Oh, you know, wracking my brain—feeding tidbits to *Señor* Garrulous over there for a sounding board—and it's bupkis as to why these things have followed us. Not *this* goddamn far."

Now Vera's watching Amos as he paces along the counter, his forehead crunched in thought.

"Curious," she says.

Doug alternates between her and Amos. "What? *What?*"

"Look at him. He's been that way for a week going."

After mulling it over, a shrugged, "He's moody," tumbles from Doug.

Vera's head slowly shakes. "Nah. More than moody. All last week—all that pestering the advanced B-group and Dr. Volkov to speed up his pheromone trials. The serum gets administered to the…fucking *plants* we've obviously never seen, and a day later, Amos goes from everyday intense-determined to fucking humbled. I didn't think that was humanly possible for him."

Doug, still at a loss: "Paint it for me like I'm five."

An abrupt sigh from Vera. "It means, we should just ask him…"

Right then she catches Amos's gaze bearing right on them, as if he'd sensed he was the subject of their little huddle, so Vera throws caution to the wind and openly waves him over. He's barely seated before Vera starts talking.

"Douglas and I were just wondering, you know, as everyday people do, how aggressive fucking kiddie-creatures managed to track us down a hundred miles away. Now, I know you're chummy with B-group, who are but a whisper removed from the haz-matted A-guys inside the vault, which means you definitely know more than we do, so out with it before I start dribbling pee in this chair."

Amos pans the room to verify the others are still watching the eyes outside watching them, then crosses a leg over the other and rolls up his pant leg to mid-shin. The bandage around his calf is a shoddy job, surely cinched on the fly and not checked since, for the blood has saturated it through. He rolls the pant leg back down.

"During the breech, one of them zipped by and just managed to graze me as I was running. I was lucky. But it paused. Sniffed the air before taking off after someone else running by. Probably figured me for incapacitated, leaving me to scavenge later. My guess is that I imprinted on it."

Doug is frowning, running his own private calculations. "Last pheromone tests in the plants topped off at a fifty-mile reaction response range…"

Vera silences him by gripping his arm, then bores into Amos. "The Volkov test last week. What were its proposed estimates?"

Realization blunts Amos's normally flinty features. "He touted a hundred-and-fifty-mile efficiency. But it was yet to be tested."

Doug lowers his head. "Crap…"

"Well, you can shake his hand and buy him dinner," Vera says, "because it's a raging fucking success. *If* his hand is still attached to him and he's not in fifteen fucking pieces spread all over a lab floor…"

"They're gone," Smiles' now familiar tuba-tone declares. "For now."

All eyes swivel to the windows to verify for themselves.

"Probably a preemptive signal," Amos says. "Letting us know it would be a waste of time for us to make a run for it."

"That's comforting, Doc, thank you," Hooch says, laying his gun back on the counter.

Amos doesn't glance back. Rather, he dwells some on Jill and Blue in their own nervous, private congregation. "If it's locked on me, then they won't stop till I'm dead. When it comes down to it, I'll lead them away so you can all make a break. Get to Fort Greely. Tell them everything."

Vera gawps at the man she's always respected, but never felt fully accepted by. She wonders if it's just her, or did everyone else receive the same stand-back vibes. "Yeah, fuck that. We're not just leaving you."

"When it comes down to it, you're not going to have a choice."

"I'm not abandoning *anybody*. Not anymore—"

Amos's glare freezes her more than any ensuing word.

"It's not about *us* anymore. These things must be stopped. Contained. And whether you like it or not, we may be the only ones left alive who have even a base understanding of what we're dealing with." Once more he's drawn to Jill and Blue, except now they're both looking back at him with muted expectation. He turns back to his cohorts. "In the interest of quelling all our combined anxiety, I'm going to try to put the owners at ease."

He rises and starts over, and to his surprise, Vera follows.

Jill tries to smile at their approach, but her lips fail her. "I've never been this scared in my life," she says as they settle around her and Blue.

Amos straightens as if called before a judge. "I'd like to apologize…"

"*We* would like to apologize," Vera cuts in.

"For bringing this mess to your doorstep," Amos resumes. "We truly had no idea what we were dealing with, and certainly didn't mean to involve anyone not affiliated with it."

Vera edges between Amos and Jill, her arms loosely hugging her belly as if she'd overeaten, though she hasn't had anything since a power bar for breakfast. "We're truly sorry for your employees."

Blue finally glances their way. A tight but appreciative grin in Vera's direction wiggles through his beard.

Jill wipes at her nose. "Thank you. It's funny: Blue and I always thought this place would be the death of us…"

They all share a delayed, sullen chuckle. Even Amos's face cracks its tension, suddenly thankful that Vera had tagged along. His gaze wanders and he sees that Doug has migrated back near Smiles. To his right, Hooch is Morse-Code-tapping the edge of a coaster against the countertop, no doubt listening in from afar while trying to pretend he's not.

"How long have you had this place?" Vera asks.

"Oh, going on twenty-five years now," Jill says. "Part of our…retirement plan. This seventy-year-old diner, originally built in Fairbanks, Alaska. Some nutty firm of Canadian developers bought it and pried it from its roots, convinced by some truth they saw as universal that all people yearn for a slice of unspoiled Americana nostalgia. And for a while, this transplanted joint did well, holding to the name The 59er until it bellied-up after 2008. The American recession wiped out most of the developers' Stateside holdings. It was then sold for pennies-on-the-dollar to the Kissells. Yours truly: Alfred "Blue" and Jill. Well, we changed the name, updated the signage, and redecorated the interior to a décor more befitting the…*hinterlander* spirit, and thus it has endured till today."

Blue's smile had flattened throughout. An incongruity that stands out like a wart on his face, Vera notes, along with her realization that the stains on his beard are actually dried paint he'd missed cleaning.

"Didn't think we'd still be slinging hash in our seventies," resumes Jill. "But mistakes were made. Presumptions and…miscalculations."

"I'm gonna make us all dinner," Blue mutters, then starts for the kitchen without meeting Jill's gaze. Vera, noticing the inconsistency of ignoring his wife's tacit approval, follows him.

"Happy to help," she says.

Now alone with Jill, Amos is swamped anew by the same dread he felt in approaching them moments earlier before Vera thawed the impending summit. Jill seems unperturbed. She rests eyes on him with practiced ease— a quarter-century of rapport-building with customers has either cultivated or augmented an already present fearlessness in butting up the supposed windows to the soul with the curtains whipped fully back.

"So, Doctor, are you a married man?"

His lips press out their color. Worse—he sees that *she* sees that.

"Not anymore," he says, and just as quickly offers a buffer he wishes he could reel right back: "You two have any children?"

Jill's mouth parts in an aborted sigh and her gaze swivels to the register in some private mustering before resuming. "We had a son. Kevin. He…died right before we bought this place. Drunk driver."

"I'm…sorry."

"I appreciate that. And you? Any little ones?"

Precisely what he feared.

"Had a boy. He was diagnosed with terminal leukemia. Lost him several years ago. *Saul.* It's what finally sank an already floundering marriage."

To his relief, Jill doesn't frown pity or offer performative consolation. She merely gazes out the window, her own thoughts percolating away.

"I don't think most people understand the…processing involved. How losing a child can kick the legs right out from under a marriage. To this day I have no clue how Blue and I managed to survive it."

Amos joins her in window-gazing. He nods at the snow corkscrewing horizontally against the glass. "Early for this level of blow, isn't it?"

Jill sniffs the gambit, but plays along. It's what keeps the customers returning, and despite Amos's charm and subtle handsomeness that has caught her off-guard already once or twice—he blends a young Alec Guinness with Peter Cushing—and despite a certain childlike innocence in the manner he self-embraces, she would happily lose this particular patron when all is said and done. "After the scorching, record-breaking summer we just had, it surely is."

And just like that, Amos concedes that he's no match.

"My wife, she tried to hide the pregnancy as long as she could. We both went into the marriage not wanting children. We were very content in our place. Happy with our careers and autonomy. Not exactly fans of where the world's headed and not wishing to burden a life that never even asked for…" His eyes alight back on hers. The least he could do is be respectful to the soul that got him to spill. "Didn't want to transmit my wonky brain issues to a child. To burden it with added obstacles in an already difficult enough life. Didn't have much of a childhood myself. My parents ran me through higher level schools once I started testing off the charts. I graduated college at 15. Guidance counselors from all over the world were as present in my life as my mother and father. Moreso, in fact. One of them even joked that I should be put out to stud and make the world smarter.

Anyway…" His chuckle staggers out like a drunk being escorted from a bar. "Of course, I fell in love with Saul the moment I saw him. It's when I became inescapably acquainted with the magic of a baby. How it turns all your frayed, kinked, overstretched nerves into harp strings, if only for a moment. Problem is, some of us are pretty tone deaf. That's the cruelty though, right? All the cold logic of everything pointing indisputably against the notion of adding passengers to an already sinking ship, and all it takes is one gander at chubby baby-folds."

Jills mouth maintains a perfect horizon. "That it does."

"She never shared with me all the early ultrasounds. The tests. Everything that revealed all the grim complications at work. Not my emotional hangups necessarily, but her family cancer history. What *she* dreaded. When I asked her about it afterward, she pretty much expressed the same surrender as mine. Seeing him on the screen as the doctor passed the probe. She said the old-soap stink of the ultrasound gel, which *lingered* for days after, became for her the personification of *baby*. For me, the smell of talcum and formula soon embodied deception, weakness, the stench of…disease. In any case, I could've done better…"

Before he knows it, Jill has grabbed his hand. He jerks at first, but her grip is more confident than anything he could sling in the moment.

"I'm sorry too," she says.

She moves off then, and he retreats to the table his group had sat at. The mutual, painless dissolution feels almost refreshing.

***

Blue expertly takes up two pots and pans in each hand, arrays them on their proper burners, and gets some water boiling.

"I figure some quick stir-fry noodles will do us good. Tossed with some chicken and veggies."

Vera, leaning cross-armed against the fridge, smiles. "Sounds lovely. Can I chop?"

From a side shelf, Blue pulls out an old cutting board mottled and hewn over decades, dumps a cluster of carrots and celery on it, and slides it across the ceramic worksurface to Vera, followed by a cleaver. "Have at it, young lady."

"*Vera*," she says, rolling up her sleeves, her nose twitching at the oddly pungent aroma of the vegetables.

Blue fully locks eyes with her. She feels safe, albeit scared and needing the distraction. She feels like an ally. "Vera it is. 'Tis a lovely name."

She starts on the carrots, hacking away the greens first. "If you don't mind me saying, Blue, you're handling all this pretty damn well, all things considered."

He slaps a pair of chicken breasts on the counter and stares at them as if they just asked for a moment longer to peck at the earth before the cleaver drops. "Don't know any other way. Art calms me. I guess it's all an extension of that. Something happens that starts to work the nerves, I'll just look at one of my paintings and go through the process of its creation: the notebook sketch, the canvas sketch, the color mixing, the base coats, the shades and highlights. Before I know it, I'm Buddha with a beard and an Appalachian accent, and not Alfred Blue Kissell, ex-jazz musician and daydreamer."

They commence their mutual chopping and slicing. Vera starts with straight cuts, then shifts to diagonal carrot slices, then stops to stretch out a fast knot in her back. "I actually had some pretty decent art talent as a kid myself, but my parents went above and beyond to dissuade me from wasting time on *hobbies*. 'Focus on *real* schoolwork, lest you become just some housewife...' Whatever. Anyway, what I'm trying to say is that I envy your outlet."

Blue's hands perfectly cube chicken, even as his eyes wander everywhere but. "You could've still done it. You know, on the side. Still can now."

Vera lets her knife tip skate figure-eights around the chopped carrots. Her eyes amble to the upright piano and the jackalope perched on a wooden base, and she pictures a hunched Blue in some dusty, tool-lined garage carefully gluing antlers and having the time of his life. Around his wife, his insecurities give off an odor—dank and peaty, like something prematurely buried trying to claw its way back to light. But in his element, he works with the confidence of a knight. "I had a chance—a moment while waiting for college apps—to run off with a kind of commune who eventually established a cool and thriving art colony that ultimately produced several famous artists. But last minute I... You know, the road not taken and all that tired aphorism horseshit. Pardon my French."

Something of a chirp croons out of Blue, and when he smiles askance at Vera, a conspiratorial twinkle fires in both eyes.

"You're in Canada, young lady. *Vera*. Some French is allowed. Hell, even fucking encouraged sometimes." He indicates at her cutting board with his knife. "And I'm partial to those julienned thin as cat whiskers."

For the first time since the calamity of this morning, Vera allows a bashful grin to freely roam. "Cat whisker thin, coming up."

***

Jill unbuttons and sheds her flannel shirt, fluttering out the damp gray t-shirt beneath. It's become ungodly hot, reminding her of the vaunted *summer-without-end* they'd just experienced. She takes note of the everyone's place, their positions on the board: Doug floating about the large man, Smiles, like a stray cat trying to curry favor and a home. Amos alone at the table, encased in his own compunctions and schemes.

And then Hooch, who like her has been surveying the space and everyone's whereabouts within it.

Their eyes meet. Neither averts. Jill finds that both laudable and infuriating. She admires confidence, but draws the line at presumption. This is *her* place, and he and his mesomorph of a partner have tried to plant their flag in it.

She starts for him. Hooch's hand involuntarily drifts to the gun on the counter but pulls right back as if trying to pilfer a cookie while mom's still in the kitchen.

"If you're still expecting that apology for disrupting your day, lady, the jury is still out."

Jill settles in close, leaning an elbow on the countertop. "Just checking in. The way I take you've been checking in on all our conversations this whole time?"

A diffident shrug. "Guilty as charged. Amazing how sound travels in a quiet diner. I will, however, apologize for your son. Couldn't even begin to imagine such a loss. Fucking boozers. Waste of space and oxygen."

An echoed shrug from Jill. "I've found there's usually an underpinning or two to that boozing that's hard to overcome."

Hooch hitches up in his stool. "That's *way* more forgiving than I could ever be."

Jill's gaze wanders across her shoulder. To Blue in the kitchen engaged with Vera. She feels the still vibrant keens of jealousy stirring awake in her depths, but in other more subtle strains than the sexual. Trust, opportunity, release. The drag of helplessness is no different though, and soon she coasts back to Hooch.

"Before this, Blue and I lived in Chicago. I worked for a Fortune-500 company under the CFO. It was high-pressure, time-consuming work, and to relieve this pressure, I found a shot of whiskey did wonders about an hour after a single diazepam. By then, Blue and I were dealing with the mood swings of an unplanned teenager we had late in life. A teenager who was also discovering drink and its compelling gifts for…muddling time and accountability."

Hooch's brow pulses. "Oh, I know that well. Grew up with a pair of drunks for parents. Had to get drunk myself to forget I sprang from those fermented loins."

Jill tries to gnaw away a smile. "Were they drunk when they named you?"

"Yeah, you're a smart-enough lady to know Hooch is not my real name."

"You and your partner go by fake names while wearing other people's names on your shirts. That's a whole lot of deception to carry around."

For a moment Hooch isn't sure if she's being sarcastic, or now just plain insulting, and the hand lingering by his gun rises to thumb the nametag on his shirt. "That's the hazard of the job." The thumb then shifts to just above his heart. "*Hooch* is the safety net from the hazards of prison life. See, on the inside, you need to find ways to make yourself…*indispensable*, lest you end up becoming something less than a man real fast. In Smiles' case, that's pretty obvious, and for him, inborn: the less smiling you do, the less you draw attention, which is a big no-no on the inside, from either cons or guards. In my case—thanks, ironically, to my sozzled parents—I nurtured a gift for crafting really damn good toilet moonshine. You hear the saying, don't shoot the messenger? Well, on the inside, it's don't shoot the barkeep. See, the names and the talents find themselves and stick. The names and the talents kept you alive. The deceptions become easy to bear after that. Like a rucksack full of cotton balls."

"Well, someone stuffed bricks in mine," Jill says, her smile turning wistful again. "One especially weighty brick was finding out your seventeen-year-old son has befriended and bedded your boss's daughter. The additional perils of company picnics no one tells you about, yes? So, the whiskey and pill rations go up. Not just for momma, but for junior too. See, beyond the usual perks, he also found a real communion with this girl. A communion in private, shared pain." Her eyes shut then as if reacting to a loud sound, and a mitigating hand promptly rises. "Check that. Pain we should've done better to have asked about. Not ignored. Not…dismissed as common teenage angst. An ache Blue was more familiar with. But I…overrode all possible interventions with the tried-and-true balm of old-fashioned gumption. Of pushing through at all costs."

Hooch, despite trying not to, keeps looking about as if beset by mosquitoes. "Why are you telling me all this?"

Even more unintentional gaffes: his words seep out as whispers.

As with Hooch's tone, Jill's inflating shoulders are also purely subconscious, and thus regrettable. She isn't sure why she'd brought any of this up initially, but it's too late now to respool all that disgorged tape.

"Because, one night, after we got into a fight about me not understanding him or his plight, Kevin tied one on something awful, stole his girlfriend's father's Aston Martin—with her help—and proceeded to joyride themselves into a telephone pole at ninety-miles-an-hour." She watches Hooch settle back in an unconscious recoil, as if to a dog he wasn't all that confident around. "Needless to say, I lost my career after that. The ensuing civil lawsuit basically crippled Blue and me. With Kevin still a minor, he was our responsibility, legal and otherwise. Anyway, Blue had a small inheritance from a grandparent. We left the states and put it into this place. It's helped some, the remove of it all. I quit drinking. Not a drop in nearly a quarter-century, and going. Some days it's…even worth it."

The anger is real and fast—it sizzles everywhere, sprouting fresh dew on his crown—but Hooch can't pinpoint the source. Like picking an individual voice at a screaming boxing match. It's his fallback whenever cornered emotionally. Yet another quirk House took the liberty of pointing out all too quickly into their friendship.

"So now here's where I'm supposed share my odious tale?" he asks. "That how this works?"

Jill's eyes quiver back, bottom lids puddling. "You can do whatever the hell you want, *Hooch*. You pretty much already have. I'm going to fix some peppermint tea. I can bring you a cup if you'd—"

"This where I tell you that for years, I tried to get my drunk mom away from my more drunk dad? Where I tell you that, intervention after intervention, it ended up with me trading fists with *Daddy* one night after a record-breaking bender? Where I tell you that my own three-sheets-to-the-wind, unthinking ass left him crippled and unable to earn a living? Where I tell you that the worst part of it all was how afterward, my mom basically disowned *me* because I ruined all her financial means, never mind all the beatings and all the verbal abuse that came with a weekly twenty-four pack? Is this what you want, *Jill?*"

His ensuing swallow is loud and all-encompassing, even prompting Amos at his table to turn for a quick look back, and Jill and Hooch glare at one another against the ubiquitous shooshing of driving snow and whistling wind until at length, Hooch relents, at which point Jill reaches up and pats his hand inches from his gun.

"I don't approve at all of what you and your partner have done and are doing here, but I'll fix you some peppermint tea anyway."

She turns away just in time to screen the first sluice of quiet tears plummeting down her cheeks, and only when she reaches the coffee-and-tea station past the register that she finally wipes them off with a countertop napkin. Upon dabbing her eyes, she just catches Amos's dropping back down into his lap after filching his glance at her moment. She nonetheless keeps her glare riding on him and Hooch beyond, who's taken to losing himself in the storm outside and who, despite wanting to convey patient fortitude, can't keep twitchiness and a persistent lip-smacking dry mouth at bay—the polar opposite of his partner, for whom no gesture is wasted. Smiles' every move or word, however minute, reads billboard gigantic—especially the slow glance he spared their way during Hooch's diatribe about his drunk parents. As if he'd just learned that fact about his partner himself.

Damn those two for coming here and capsizing her world, she thinks. Her *space*. And those three government scientists as well for bringing their unholy creations to her front door. Are they even aware of their coarse intrusion? Do they even feel—

A sudden yelp and a flurry of muttered curses spring from the kitchen, and only then does Jill realize she's standing by the wall mere inches before the pass-through counter starts.

Inches from Blue and Vera.

"Dammit, I knew it," she hears Vera say, and Jill carefully edges an eye around the wall to spy the goings on.

Vera is pinching a bleeding thumb over the floor while Blue fetches the first-aid kit by the refrigerator.

"Sorry to be a bother," she says, adding a playful growl for emphasis.

Blue opens the kit and fishes out some gauze and band aids. "No, no. Gotta speak up. No shame there."

"I grew up in a Latin household, where everyone spoke up—*loud*—except for what they really needed."

Upending some hydrogen peroxide on a cotton pad, Blue proceeds to dab at Vera's cut thumb, which she groans and grits her teeth through.

"Loud and aggressive gobbledygook is easier than whispered basics," Blue says, taking up the gauze and unwinding a generous length. "Should be the other way around. Learned that the hard way. But more internalized, less aggressive natures tend to yield against louder, more aggressive ones who think they know better simply because they're louder and more aggressive. Alas, we're upright and not very bright."

A grin tempers Vera's scowl. "Get the fuck out of here—an artist *and* a poet?"

Blue's ever-present sheepish grin. "Watch your French, young lady."

"Fuck my French, old man!"

They dissolve into a mutual giggle fit, with Blue struggling to wind the gauze around her finger while she labors equally and fruitlessly to hold still.

Unbeknownst to them, an eavesdropping Jill smiles, drifts back to the coffee station, and fights in vain against a fresh onslaught of tears while ripping open teabags. Contentment, jealousy, pride—they all dryer-tumble in her belly at once.

She's about to pour hot water into mugs when the flicker catches her attention—a series of blinks from outside before all the parking lot lights snuff out at once, and all turns black.

***

"Oh man," someone utters through the darkness—Doug being the consensus of most—before a chorused, *"Everyone stay calm,"* issues from the duet of Hooch and Amos.

Only the ghostly, sponged ambience from the snow etches some form to the objects and people inside the diner, and as a result all eyes drift to the windows.

"Please tell me it's not them who cut off the power," Vera says. She and Blue join the others in the dining area after a few hip bumps against jutting counters, including one nasty bump on the piano from Vera that twirls the jackalope like a bowling pin before catching and righting itself as if alive and slighted.

Amos, who'd risen once the lights went out, has wound his way by feel through the dining room, ending up by the corner booth he and his cohorts initially occupied. He squints out the window, scanning for the dead blue of eyes. "It's probably the storm. Jill, do you have generator backup?"

"We do," she says. "But it's old and takes a bit to kick on."

"The fuck is that?"

Smiles. All heads snap in his direction in time to see him shoulder his rifle before looking out the window again.

"I don't see anything," says Doug.

"*Listen*," Smiles growls.

And soon they all start hearing it. Gradually above the shrilling wind, what is first taken as the high-pitched chitter of coyote song soon transmutes into something more familiar and far more unsettling, and the collective denial of it quickly sloughs away to indisputable fact: the nearby giggling of mischievous children.

"Please stop that…" Vera tells the windows, hugging her churning belly tighter.

It's close, almost inside the room, and when they see the movement, it's all at once—a mass revelation of an optical illusion puzzle.

Silhouettes of long-fingered hands reaching up, probing atop the outside windowsills like spider legs just above where the booths back against the glass along the storefront.

"Fuck me," Smiles mumbles, just as the playground giggling outside crests, and several of the creatures bound away from the diner and back into the trees.

He takes aim with his rifle only to lower it once the immediate threat has passed. Seconds later, the parking lot lights flare back on as one.

"Oh my god," Doug manages to say before doubling over and dry-retching.

"Jesus," Smiles whispers.

For everyone else, the sight manifests in the slow development of Polaroids. Some greet what they see with gasps, others with groaned curses—and even then, they're not quite prepared to accept its reality.

Spaced along the windowsills, almost perfectly equidistant from each other, are the exhumed eyeballs of the recently slaughtered, the roots of their optic nerves fluttering like windsocks against the gales.

5

THERE ARE EIGHT eyes in total.

The two cooks and the two hikers.

Upon taking in the naked, dilated orbs, Amos retreats from the storefront, his heart thumping in his throat, hands fumbling behind himself for the table he occupied before the lights went out. The collective held-breath of the room spreads its weight, distributing mass so as not to break through fragile, splintering ice.

"What the hell animal does this?" Hooch says, shattering that sheet for better or worse. "This is…"

"Intimidation," Smiles finishes for him. His rifle is still partially elevated, its muzzle end a Richter-scale needle during a mild temblor.

"So they're…*taunting* us?" Vera says. She hasn't been able to shed the sensation of tiny bug feet scrambling atop her skin or burrowing into her marrow in helixed galleries since the first attack, and now her belly has joined in the squirm.

"In a manner of speaking."

Doug, after a good throat-clearing, wipes his mouth and attempts vainly to flatten and straighten out his sweaty shirt.

"Well, it's fucking working," Vera says. "In a *manner of speaking.*"

Smiles lets his barrel arc to the floor. "Some animals employ the tactic."

"Sure…" Doug says, and again coughs out the frog. "But even…the pursuit of, say, orcas, is simply to tire out prey. We just see it as cruel and even sadistic. If anything, some prey animals tend to preemptively swarm a potential predator with sheer numbers to dissuade them from attacking."

"Chimpanzees," Smiles offers.

Doug nods to no one in particular. His face remains ashen and his eyes quiver like boxers attempting to stand after a solid roundhouse to the jaw. "Primates have been known to employ actual malice stemming from…insecurity, spite. Even vengeance."

"This is simple, garden-variety childhood provocation."

Everyone turns to Amos. He's sitting again at his table, cradling his elbows, neck more drawn within his shoulders. "They're *goading* us," he adds. "Seeing if we take their bait. Seeing if one of us is bullish enough to step outside our bubble."

Once more Jill recognizes the child of him, only now she reproaches herself for it, as if letting sympathy leak for a repeat abuser. "You know what they are, don't you?"

Air streams from Amos's sharp nose, flaring his nostrils and twisting the corners of his mouth in conflicting directions. Even in stillness, a fitful aura judders from his eyes; twin jitterbugging lids atop pots just starting to boil.

"They're called Outcrosses. *Unofficially.* Their actual designation thus far is merely a string of numbers, but some are working to craft an actual Latin taxonomic categorization."

All gazes settle on him as various-slot machine windows. For Jill and Blue, they flutter to a stop on fear and condemnation. For Doug and Vera, it's shocked betrayal. For Hooch and Smiles, it's inexorable, expected subterfuge finally unfurling naked to the floor.

Dense silence once more threatens to drag the room under until again it's Hooch who smashes it.

"Fucking eggheads."

Amos swallows a caustic globule of freshly expelled hormones. "Please direct all future vitriol to me and me alone. Doug and Vera didn't know the level of their involvement."

No sooner are his words out than he watches them both unconsciously sidle closer together. How he'll ever manage to adequately apologize to them is a matter for a later time.

"Weaknesses?" Smiles prompts.

The attention from his left allows Amos to switch his already cramping injured leg so he could centralize himself better to the group. He wipes his brow of sweat with some napkins and draws a breath that trips on the way in. This wasn't anything he ever expected to divulge. Nothing he ever rehearsed for.

"Their skin is crafted from nanocrystals imbued into an organic and carbon fiber latticework over the musculature to maintain a near-perfect ectothermal and endothermal balance. Surgically modified reverse-hinged knees for faster, more efficient quad-pedal locomotion. An ability to filter saltwater, as well as metabolize the water from whatever they eat in times of severe scarcity. Lungs better-suited to tolerate higher carbon dioxide levels. Eyes better-equipped to see at night and in higher spectrums. The employment of specific predator DNA markers, in addition to tardigrade DNA to augment the ability to endure harsh environments—extreme cold, heat, pressure. Possibly even the vacuum of space, though that's yet to be tested."

He glances at Doug and Vera, their arms clutching to each other now like siblings lost in the woods, their gazes searching the ground for elusive maps that will guide them away from the horrors.

"Designed and built for all contingencies, from near-future climate calamities to farther-future planetary relocation. Still, they're not impervious to extraneous technology. Bullets *will* kill them. And, having been designed to adapt over days or even hours instead of minutes, any rapid transitions in temperature will render them the weakest and most vulnerable while they readapt. Hence our toasty little bubble. Speaking of which, we should consider supplemental heat sources in case we have another blackout, storm-generated or otherwise. If we can prepare to quickly start a contained fire somehow…"

He looks about through a bemused squint for some solution to present itself until a soft voice speaks up from behind.

"We got a Hibachi grill in the back."

Blue.

Jill snaps a quick look in his direction before her eyes trickle to the floor again.

"For cookouts on warm days after work and the like," resumes the old man. "The kitchen was oriented different when we bought the place. They had the grill located roughly where the register is now. The old flue is still up there above the ceiling panels, just duct-taped over. Also have the old range hood in the back which I kept for some…future art project. Wouldn't take long to reattach it. We can slide the grill right under it."

Amos levels him a thin smile that nonetheless hums with gratitude. "That's an excellent idea, Blue."

Blue dips his head in accord and heads to the back, but not before pausing to give Jill's shoulders a fond squeeze against which she yieldingly, lovingly cants her head.

"Babies…"

It's Vera. The word wanders out. An unsure response against a dwindling, quiz-show clock.

"I...try to look at the irony that these abandoned, terminal babies who've taxed the resources of those who'd cast them aside to starve on the streets, may now become humanity's salvation," Amos says, knowing even as he started that he was shooting spitballs at a 500-pound charging gorilla.

Vera doesn't meet his gaze. She just shakes her head before pivoting from Doug's loose embrace and marching to the back to help Blue.

"Or our destruction."

Hooch. Old faithful when it comes to killing silences.

"There's no irony here, Doc. Just a failure in family planning. I pretty much said the same to my old man before he kicked me out of the house at fourteen."

"Maybe he deserved it," Amos says.

Though muttered in a distracted fugue, the words spur Hooch off his stool. He storms up to Amos and looms.

"That's not for you to say, Doc. Not one fucking bit."

"Hooch, please..." starts Jill, only for Hooch to cut her down with a sickled glower.

Amos shoots Hooch a glimpse. "We should listen to the lady—"

Hooch hauls him off his seat with two fistfuls of shirt, toppling his chair and rattling the condiments on the table into colliding Weeble Wobbles.

***

"Where are your tools?" Vera asks, pinching her nose against the new sting of mildew and solvents.

Blue is hunched over at a corner of the office-slash-storeroom-slash-human-sized-junk-drawer, dragging away precarious, slumped towers of file boxes. "In the closet right behind you. Top shelf."

She tiptoes to drag out the red toolbox, and as she brings it down has to plop it quickly on a work counter lest she drop it from the sudden cramp that gores her side.

"When are you due?" Blue asks, exhuming the rust-teared vent hood from where it has rested in the corner for decades.

Vera grits her teeth against pain, surprise, and shame. "How...the hell do you know that?"

Blue flits modest eyes her way before wiping down the hood with a rag. "Jill had the same symptoms before she knew herself. The cramps, the sensitivity to smells. All four pregnancies were the same. Was the worst with the only one that actually took. The only one we hadn't planned... Dammit!"

A discordant plucked note jangles as Blue pulls his hand from the split wedge of metal on the hood that snagged flesh along the meaty section of hand below his pinky. Almost at once a long seam of blood beads and slivers to the floor. He plucks the cleanest rag from the counter and presses it against the cut.

Vera backs into a counter to bend away the alternating jabs to her sides. "The father doesn't know yet. Obviously, no one I work with does either, and I gotta keep it that way."

A length of dusty vent pipe in one hand, Blue gives Vera a hush-hush zipper-lip with his other.

She smiles through another pang, this one cycling around her entire midriff. "I don't know if I want this, Blue."

Blue shrugs. It's a grandfather's gesture, brimming with sagacity and amused boredom. "We weren't sure we wanted Kevin either. He came late in life to us, see? So, we were faced with a now-or-never scenario. I still don't know if we chose wisely, but we chose. And that's what you can do too. Just know that if you do, you can't half-ass it. That said...you've got time and youth yet."

Vera unconsciously mirrors his shrug. "Time is the problem now, isn't it? No one knows how much they have. People just assume they all have a full tank of it, with plenty of road ahead of them. Especially the *youth*."

Blue nods. He grabs the next cleanest rag available after the first has sopped through with blood and wraps it around his hand. "All I know? Damn thing runs slow early, runs fast late. Now let's get this thing up and running, yeah? We can discuss time later at our leisure when we have more of it."

"Goddamn poet," Vera says, and snorts.

He taps the side of his nose, leaving a vague rosy blood smudge. "Don't tell Jill. One artistic indulgence is already too much for her. Now, if you can drag the grill, I'll take the hood and the tools."

***

"Since we're in this fucking mess because of you," Hooch seethes inches from Amos's face, his hands white from the pressure of holding the man off the floor just by his shirt, "maybe we should just toss your ass outside. Use you as bait so the rest of us can slip out the back."

Jill marches over and tries in vain to wedge herself between them. "Put him down!" she snarls. She's shocked by her own anger; it's been so long since it free-ranged.

Such is the implication to Hooch as well, for he relents his hold, but only enough for Amos's toes to find the ground again.

It's all Amos needs to catch his breath.

"We should listen…to Jill. Because the Outcrosses are drawn to anxiety. Cortisol, specifically. Humans are excellent producers—better than animals because the animal fight-flight response is momentary. Humans let theirs linger. And these beings…they were created under an umbrella of future dreads, so I suggest we remain as calm and placid as possible."

Hooch gnaws on his rage a beat longer before releasing Amos with a shove, then stomps back to his spot at the counter.

"Everything okay?" Vera asks. She and Blue pause at the threshold of the dining room, an old grill, a rusted range hood, and some tools distributed amongst them.

Amos throws her a curt nod before righting his chair and sitting back down.

A green-in-the-gills Doug shambles to help Vera and Blue, and Jill gravitates nearby as they set up to work by the register. Smiles drifts to Hooch to confab over whatever felons do whenever the shit hits their fan.

Amos's thoughts drift to his no-longer son. His tiny hands and feet. His cowlick of auburn hair, so like his mother's. How could he ever explain to these people here—and by dint, the world entire—that he did this all for them? That he did it all for Saul?

***

It takes them over an hour to complete the fireplace, with Vera and Doug taking over the work after Blue's instructions so that he can finish preparing dinner.

After perfunctorily eating a supper that otherwise would've garnered praise for its simplicity and goodness, the Hibachi grill is dragged under the new hood. Amos suggests using the cleanest material possible to burn after Jill returns with a red gas can from the back. That clean, unlacquered wood or even paper is a preferable fuel. That the initial smoke before the flue draws it out would be toxic otherwise. Hooch chuckles at the quibble, but nonetheless aids by cracking the legs off some old stools in the back and helping to stoke the flames under the grill, and soon everyone sheens in unctuous sweat, settled equidistant from the improvised hearth and the storefront.

**

It's close to midnight when sapphire eyes begin winking again from the tree line. As before, they appear and reappear in random locations and planes. Smiles threatens to crack open the door to take a few potshots.

"If you can't verify center-mass," Amos says, "you'd just be wasting your ammunition. They could be peering from around trees, or hanging from them, and your shots will just fly harmlessly past them into the woods."

No one says it, but the collective dread is that the Outcrosses, as Amos referred to them, would just child-giggle at them afterward, augmenting the very anxiety that acts as lure.

Over the next hour, irregular, troubling sounds shudder everyone to attention, just as the monotony of waiting without anything to do anchors them to their seats and thoughts. Sounds of scratches and tapping on the walls, skittering on the roof. The latter is particularly disarming, the high ground advantage an instinctive dread even in humans.

"Heat rises and the attic is the hottest part of the diner," Doug says, in an attempt to mollify the unease. "Besides, if they're going to gung-ho barge in to tear us apart, they'd simply crash through the glass."

"They're just testing structural integrity," Amos says, in an attempt to mollify Doug's tactlessness. "We should be solid."

"Hot as fucking Houston in here," Hooch says. Despite Doug's undisputable observation, his eyes still scan the ceiling nonetheless, hand spidered atop the gun on the counter.

"Jacksonville," counters Smiles, and the two exchange glances of practiced ribbing they're too hot to extend any further.

Sensing the collective malaise, Blue rises and announces he'll make some coffee to keep everyone alert. Fresh blood wicks to the floor between his feet from the still angry cut in his hand, and he stoppers it with a handful of dispenser napkins while grinding the spill into the floorboard gaps with the toes of his shoes.

He just settles the paper filter into the coffeemaker when lights gradually brighten outside, followed by the crunch of snow, and moments later the splash of headlights through the windows.

Smiles, having the best angle away from the blinding light, ducks down to squint out the window, and when he rises Hooch immediately spots his confusion and worry.

"What is it?"

Now everyone watches perplexed as Smiles quickly dons his police jacket and hat before barking at Hooch: "Heads up—police cruiser."

6

"SHIT," HOOCH GRUNTS, almost toppling off his stool to ready himself like Smiles. Upon zipping up his coat after using its shearling lining to mop his head of sweat, he stabs a finger at Jill before flipping it over in a come-hither beckon. "Everyone else, move away from the windows and keep cool."

Jill reassures Blue with a quick nod to continue making coffee, grabbing her coat and scarf on the way after Hooch jerks at his lapel in a manner suggesting that she also get into character fast.

"We're doing repairs," he tells her. "The eggheads are electricians. We're having power problems. Tell them that or anything else you think will send them on their way. Whatever happens, they can't come inside, you follow me?"

She sees Smiles exchange his rifle for a police-issued sidearm before looking back at Hooch. Nothing but bitter truth pickles their eyes, so she just nods at Hooch and moves for the door that Smiles proceeds to unlock.

The instant cold is a bite at first welcomed but quickly rebuffed as Jill steps one foot outside and the wind knifes instantly through the stitching of her clothes. Smiles lines himself up against the strike jamb while Hooch looms behind her.

The cruiser's driver side door opens and an officer steps out, quickly stamping his feet against the fresh ice. He rainbow waves and yells against the wind: "Hey there, Jill!"

Jill glimpses sideways against the cruiser headlights. "That you, Stan?"

The tall, round-faced officer in his fifties cranes his neck to look inside. "That it is. Hey, everything okay in there? Saw the parking lights on but not the inside lights."

"Power failure!" Jill calls back. She sees Stan's partner step out of the passenger side. Milton, the svelte, foppish rookie she met last month. Despite temps in single digits, he shucks down his parka and twists it at the hem to assure that the zipper lines up perfectly to his belt buckle. "Parking lot and the inside are on two different breakers. Got some workers on it. Plumbing problems too. Stinks like week-old roadkill in here."

Now both officers are twisting and tilting heads like owls to better understand the activity inside until both their eyes track over to the police pickup before filing back to the door, whereupon Smiles leans out and offers them a quick salute and passable grin.

"These two officers stopped by an hour ago and were nice enough to stay and help," Jill yells, hoping the crack in her voice hasn't betrayed her. "We're good here. But you two should get down this mountain ASAP!"

The older officer, Stan, at glancing about the driving snow, stiffens noticeably at spotting the odd shape protruding from the side of the road. At the same time Jill feels Hooch's grip tighten on her arm before he hisses a curt, "Get rid of 'em," in her ear.

It's the hikers' Humvee that Stan sees, last used to plow into the scientists' RAV4, sending it down the embankment, and which now sits perpendicular to the road, half on it and half on the shoulder.

Stan backs away from his cruiser, awning a hand over his eyes to better peer his suspicions at the oddly arranged vehicle before turning back to Jill. "You sure everything's okay?"

"Yeah, Stan! Too many cooks in the kitchen as is…"

Her words stumble and fall as the background flares alive with dozens of icy-blue eyes popping open in unison, followed by the rustle of undergrowth waking left-right like the wave at a stadium, and only when the first lean, springy outlines punch through the bracken does she manage to scream, "Get out of here!" before she feels herself yanked roughly back and to the floor.

Amos is already on his feet, grabbing a dumbfounded Doug by the collar and snagging Vera by the wrist and dragging them close to the Hibachi grill.

Everyone watches slack-jawed as the first Outcross—legs splayed like a cat in mid-pounce—swipes its taloned hand as it swoops down upon the older officer, Stan, ripping across the parka. Almost immediately his bicep and deltoid unfurl through the sleeve in the vein of instant crescent rolls popping from a can.

The officer barely has time to glance at his ruptured arm with the annoyance of having been bee-stung before the Outcross, already gathered on the snowy ground before him, springs back up, anchoring its hind claws into the meat of Stan's thighs before swiping its forelimbs across his face and chest in an alternating blur of fresh red rakes.

Only then does he start to scream—surprise, confusion, and agony dueling for volume rights.

The younger officer, Milton, at seeing his partner hacked to ribbons by what he can only surmise is some deformed mountain lion, clutches at his sidearm, but terror keeps it there a beat too long in a locked tremble. It remains so, even as a second Outcross leaps on him from behind and starts to claw-wring his head off at the neck.

Several more immediately wriggle from the tree line to join the melee, low to the ground in rapid feline-serpentine crouches.

The pops of gunfire ensue, muted somewhat by the howling winds and screams from Stan, whose face is nearly down to bone.

Smiles and Hooch, opening up from the door with their sidearms.

Amos hunkers down and moves to drag Jill away, herself petrified in a partial supine on the floor, upper body elevated by her elbows as if watching the surf from a beach towel.

"Shut the damn door!" Amos yells at Hooch and Smiles.

But the two keep firing. Doug and Vera watch through the windows as one Outcross takes a one-two hit to its chest, its hind legs hinging on themselves before it collapses to one side, dead.

Another takes a slug to the upper shoulder blade as it tries to swipe the leg off a still-standing-but-now-headless Milton, the impact spinning the creature toward the diner, whereupon a following shot shears off the left side of its head from the eye up. The other eye's ghostly light flickers to black before it twirls lifelessly into the snow.

Vera isn't aware she's flinching the entire time, nor that she and Doug have been unconsciously stepping closer to the windows to better see.

To see all that they'd wrought without knowing it.

As quickly as they appeared, the Outcrosses have retreated into the trees, leaving behind two of their own and the barely recognizable humps of two dead men, their mangled, twisted corpses headlight backlit and already flocked by snow.

So statue-still is everyone by the sudden quiet-after-the-storm that it takes several seconds to recognize the cracking of something wooden, followed by fresh screaming.

Several seconds more to realize it's not coming from outside, but within.

Jill's cry for help breaks the collective ice, and all eyes turn to see a hollering Blue by the coffee station, arms flailing as his entire left leg has disappeared into the floor.

He's being pulled under.

Vera is the first to move, followed by Jill then Doug.

Jill, on her knees, wraps her arms around Blue's torso while the other two take an arm and pull.

"I got this," Smiles says, shoving Hooch in Blue's direction before heaving Amos out of his way to close and bolt the door.

Blue's roars morph suddenly into shrieks as the sounds of crunching and tearing rip up through the floorboards, and suddenly Jill, Vera, and Doug effortlessly hoist Blue off the floor, his left leg gone just above the knee.

Amos lunges for the coffee station and grabs one of the carafes. He peers into the hole in the floor. Glimpses the burn of their eyes gazing back up, along with the drench of Blue's blood on their corpse-gray skin. Amos gulps old and looming reservations, then upends the carafe into the hole. Scalding water hits their flesh, steaming instantly and sending the creatures crashing and careening out of the crawlspace, their screeches both callow and wholly inhuman.

Blue's agony seeps out as wounded whale song while Hooch picks up his body and carries him to the large corner table—the booth the three scientists initially occupied. Jill follows, slipping this way and that on her husband's pumping blood. She gazes unsure at Hooch, and Hooch squeezes her shoulders and shakes her once to splinter her shock.

"I have medical training. Army. Do you have a first aid kit?"

A nod merges with a head shake in Jill. Still, more a nod than shake, and she trundles off into the kitchen.

Vera joins Hooch at the table, bringing with her an armload of towels, several of which she presses directly against the angry red stump.

Upon contact Blue's back arches off the table as if electrified, and he wolf-howls to the ceiling.

Hooch, holding down his upper body, searches out Smiles, and finds him only after he emerges from the back of the diner, a partial sheet of plywood and a drill in tow.

Doug, chin trembling, sidles away from the gore that is Blue to stand closer to Smiles, who's already at work trying to cover the hole in the floor.

Amos joins them at the table, helping Vera to staunch the bleeding. Jill returns, the first aid kit held out in a trembling hand like a heavy plate of flapjacks she's serving to a table. Vera plucks it from her and she and Amos rifle through the contents for what they need, but Hooch grabs Amos by the shoulder and snarls, "Switch," before swiping the kit from Vera and pulling out rolled gauze and a suture set with one hand as if he'd packed the kit himself.

Jill slides herself into the booth, shimmying around until she's parallel with her husband's head. She takes his hand with one of hers while her other pats his forehead. She leans close and whispers unheard comfort into his ear.

A terrible howl-squeal from Blue as Hooch pulls the blood-sodden towels from the stump. Two fast pumps of arterial flow splat on the table before Hooch presses a clean bundle against it. The stabbing against his hand from the jagged, forked femur prods a grunt from Hooch, while Amos has to lean his weight over the table to palm down Blue's writhing, growling body at his shoulders.

The sudden whine of power drill from Smiles coincides with the abrupt ceasing of Blue's thrashing, and Hooch, Vera, and Amos freeze suddenly, even as Jill continues to mouth words of soothing and apology into her husband's ear.

"Is he...?" starts Vera, but Hooch grabs her hands and presses them against the towels before swiveling himself over and pressing two fingers against Blue's neck.

A closed-eye nod, then, "Just passed out. Thankfully." He catches Amos's eye. "Gimme your belt. Then go boil some more water." Then to Vera. "You squeamish around blood?"

Vera looks up almost casually, gore sleeving her arms to the elbows, before shaking her head once. "Been conscripted as a nurse more times than I can count. The perks of volunteering in third-world countries."

Amos hands Hooch his belt, which he promptly uses to tourniquet Blue's leg. Jill is still speaking into Blue's ear, and Hooch says, "You don't have to be here for this."

She looks up and gazes at the threshold of a smile. "This is *my* husband. And this is *my* place." And she's back to whispering.

Hooch turns to Vera and orders her to wash her hands as fast as she can. He then peels open the suture kit and arranges the bits on the table before him. Just as he starts to thread a needle, a hair-raising wail from outside that seems expelled by the very mountains themselves lances through the glass.

A lone Outcross outside, its limber frame crouched over its fallen pack members, touching them in vain for signs of life. Upon seeing none, it hoists its elongated neck and issues a second soprano keen into the driving snow in a near-parody of a wolf.

"The fuck are you doing, Doc?" hisses Hooch, but it's too late.

Amos has stepped right up to the front door, hands palming the glass. Quivering eyes regard the monstrosity he created outside with the look of a parent watching their child being worked on by a frantic E.R. team.

The Outcross, as if snagging on a scent, whips its head directly toward the door and the man standing behind it. It rises deliberately, its reverse-hinged knees suggesting more height than present by dint of its uncanny, discomfiting nature.

The child-thing then canters straight for the door.

Hooch drops the needle and thread and unholsters his gun, followed by Smiles doing the same from the floor he's working to cover, but Amos slowly swings back a hand to stay their actions.

The Outcross stops ten feet short of the door's threshold, and only then does Vera gasp. Clutched against the creature's side in the manner of a running back cradling a football, the younger officer's severed head, his expression forever frozen in amazed bewilderment.

Amos and the thing he made lock eyes, the latter's stout muzzle flaring and baring its feline fangs. Everything above the mouth is soft-featured and still screams child, albeit without hair, and the contrast is nearly hobbling in its contradiction. The thing pants and seethes at the man behind the glass, and when Amos's hands stuff into his pockets, the creature roars—the sound of a boy about to leap from a couch onto a session of roughhousing already underway—before hoisting the head above its own, shaking it like an athlete would a trophy.

"Step away from the glass, Doc."

It's Hooch, but there's little authority to it. More suggestion from trepidation and dread.

But Amos holds steady.

The Outcross cants its head at the man's steadfastness, then issues a cat's hiss before bracing the head against its stomach and gouging its claws into it, hooking out the eyes, which it proceeds to hurl against the door one-two.

The orbs *thunk* against the glass, and everyone inside flinches concurrently as if being shot at.

All except for Amos, who continues to gaze solemnly back.

The Outcross snarls its retort, then starts excavating into the dead officer's mouth, at length fishing out his tongue before likewise side-arming it to the door. The organ splats against the glass, coaxing yelps from inside as it sticks and starts to worm down the pane, leaving an unctuous, reddish trail behind it before peeling away.

Only then does Amos step back.

At seeing this, the Outcross snaps a simian bark before tucking the head under an arm and dashing back into the woods.

It takes several more minutes before guns are re-holstered, power drills whine back up, and needles start threading together an amputated stump.

Amos holds by the door a good ten minutes longer, searching out form in the blackness through the driving snow.

7

THE HOURS TRUDGE.

Except for the occasional dream gurgle and spasm, Blue has remained in an unconscious feverish state, Jill unmoved from his side.

Everyone is down to undershirts, the swelter inside fever-potent and nearly unbearable. Each crackle of flame or popping knot from the Hibachi is an additional punch-to-the-gut gibe. The near-zero-degrees outside look as inviting to the denizens of the Last Chance Grill as the waters of a crystal-clear cove in Tahiti.

Aside from a few rumbled asides between Hooch and Smiles, no one has spoken since the police attack and Blue's injury, with each person staking their own area of the dining room in which to enisle themselves further from the horrendous memory of it all.

Periodically Hooch will glance at Smiles working the police scanner, eyes narrowed while both hands smother the headset against his ears. His gruff, returned headshakes are as loud as any yelled retort.

And then the sound of a swallow summits the silence—more than a commonplace mannerism—followed by the unmistakable jangle of a rifle coming to bear.

"Oh for fuck's sake," manages Vera, only to crab both hands over her mouth lest she worsen the situation.

At the corner booth, inches behind Jill's slumbering head on the table, two pairs of blazing eyes peer over the windowsill like something out of a Warner Brothers cartoon.

The Outcrosses cant their heads this way and that at the two elderly owners like mischievous kids trying to work out the least disruptive way to draw a mustache on their father napping on the couch.

Hooch, finally glimpsing the spectacle himself, stirs to grab his gun, his stool creaking loudly in the process, to which Amos stabs back a hand to cease his movements.

But the damage is done.

Jill mumbles awake, her head groaning off the table. Strands of gray hair pull taut before snapping off their anchorage in Blue's dry blood. At first her weary gaze notes her unconscious husband, especially the ruddy smudge on the side of his nose, but gradually the curdled breaths of the entire room drag her eyes up, and she catches every alarmed face glaring right back at her.

Amos mutters a terse, "Keep calm," as Jill slowly turns her head back. Because the *something-is-behind-you* implication doesn't require words, but a whole lot of angst-riddled energy to stoke it, and when her eyes meet the glowing sets of her eavesdroppers, they're only eight inches and one thin pane of glass apart.

The Outcrosses huff matching fog-bubbles on the glass, their taloned fingertips tined and flexing into the wooden sill they're peering over.

Jill's eyes widen. A squeak slips through her pressed lips, and a swallow trembles down her throat, generating a body-wide shake that slings to her feet before cycling back up, and when her mouth parts, the anticipated scream of terror is instead a mother-bear roar of fury that she holds and leans into until her forehead thumps the glass, whereupon the Outcrosses recoil, glimpse at each other in puerile accord, and sprint back to the tree line.

The subsequent fog bubble from her rage-holler overspreads the two the Outcrosses left in a Venn diagram of terror and ferocity. She gathers herself by pressing and opening her eyes multiple times before leaning over to kiss Blue's forehead. Then she rises.

She stretches her arms as if just having gotten out of bed, then walks to the piano. There she carefully moves the jackalope to one side before opening the wooden base it stood on, which was always a box, and draws out a lighter and a pack of Viceroys. Settling the jackalope back on its pedestal, she returns to the booth, taps the pack with perfect muscle-memory ease, and lights herself a smoke.

Her first drag is a yogi's practiced, meditative breath.

At one point Vera moves to the booth and, as gently as she can, leans over Jill and her squiggle of smoke, and twists the blinds closed behind her before settling into the booth herself. Without a word, Jill offers her the pack, and Vera takes one, lights it, pulls a single, long drag that reddens the cherry brake-light red before stuffing it out on the vinyl beside her.

Jill takes a few more puffs before putting out her own smoke in a like manner and nestling her head against the crook of her elbow by Blue.

She's asleep moments later, and only then do all the held breaths in the room blow out in a series of steeped gusts.

***

The first hints of blue blush the snow outside in the hue of snowy CRT televisions, so like the color of Outcross eyes. The storm has mostly passed, the snowfall outside light and almost Christmas-card cozy.

"They're gone," Smiles says.

Everyone stirs from partial slumbers to regard his large, stooped frame scanning out the windows.

"Who's gone?" Doug asks, the note of good-news prospect in his voice trilling through.

"All the bodies. Even the beasts we took down."

"Great," Doug mutters, knuckle-rubbing his eyes.

"They're hoarding the officers' remains," Amos says. "They're likely cannibalizing their own."

"Wonderful," Hooch says, a cheek nestling his palm atop an elbow kickstand on the countertop. "That's comforting, Doc, thank you."

Amos, himself yawning through a restless sleep, catches Jill's head resting atop Blue's chest, her fingers harrowing soft pleats through his paint-flecked beard. He looks calm, his fever hopefully broken.

To his right, Doug and Vera—the latter having eventually left Jill to be alone with Blue at the booth—rise and stretch before Vera moves to check on the old couple.

They can't do another night of this, thinks Amos. Blue won't make it, and neither will their nerves. His own team has held up surprisingly well considering all the bloodshed and revelations to their involvement in said bloodshed, but he can only count on shock masking their sanity for so long.

He rises through cracking joints. Coffee whispers seductively in his ear, but as he moves for the station, he's pulled by the small picture set against the top row of keys on the cash register. A picture his mind took no notice of when he stood on the very same spot last night before dumping boiling water onto crawlspace-raiding Outcrosses. A slightly younger Blue and Jill, with a moody teenager between them standing before what looks like a Christmas tree lot. The boy, Kevin, perhaps a year away from his rendezvous with destiny in the form of car-thieving joyride and immovable telephone pole. He has Jill's eyes and firm set of mouth, and Blue's wide nose and jaunty stance.

All the doled-out traits alive and vibrant in a crinkled 4x6 print.

Amos looks away. Perhaps out of shame for stealing looks at something Jill meant as private. Perhaps to not glimpse the fatalism leaking from the boy's gaze as he'd already sampled seeping from his mother.

Sampled in Saul as disease slowly taking root...

He marches straight to Hooch.

"We need to get Blue to a hospital," he says quietly. "Maybe wait another hour for the sun to come up fully and figure out a distraction of some kind. If we're lucky, we'll get some actual clear sunlight to dull their reaction time some."

Hooch pats his gun as if it were the head of a trusty, loyal mutt. "We're not going anywhere until we get our brother back."

Amos catches Smiles' glare focused their way. His ears twitch, the rifle resting on his lap like a snoozing tomcat.

"That could be hours," he says. "Blue doesn't have that."

Hooch's eyes drip molten lead. "Let's not forget why we're still here, Doc."

"So you're going to blame that storm on us?"

"No, Doc. I'm blaming those unholy things out there on you. You're the reason six people are now dead, and Blue is hanging on by a thread. Compared to that, the whims of Mother Nature are easy-breezy."

Amos's eyes go rogue on him, bouncing about the other heads in the room before dribbling back to Hooch. "None of that fixes the *now*. To stay here much longer is to kill Blue and plunge the rest of us deeper in the creek."

"Ever abandon someone you took for dead, Doc, only to realize you...*erred?*"

Not the response from Hooch that Amos anticipated, nor the response within himself at the posed question: remorse. His only physical reply is a single headshake.

"Well, that's why Smiles and I are here. We fucked up, and now our brother is doing twenty-to-life because of said fuck-up, and we aim to make amends of this fuck-up, come hell or high water. Or, in this case, fucking nightmare monster brats made by nutcases."

Amos sighs, then plants a foot on the stool rung between Hooch's legs. Before the other can foment on the intrusion, Amos rolls up his pant hem and bares the wound, the sloppy gauze-work already rust-browning. "That's my fuck-up," he says before putting his foot back down. "One of them cut me at the lab, and they followed my scent here. Comes the moment we need to make our break, I'll bait them away. All I ask in return is that you get Doug and Vera down the mountain."

Hooch's grin, despite his sweaty, reddened face, could dry wet clothing.

"Just like that, huh, Doc? You'll just let everyone go their separate ways after your ultra-top-secret government experiment blew up in your face and is now running wild in the Yukon? Forgive me if I remain…incredulous."

Amos's brow cambers, generating frown lines that can be sown with seed.

"Because you and your cell buddy are innocent victims here trapped by simple happenstance? We're both yoked to culpability. The way I see it, all we have to run on is a mutual *you-go-your-way-we-go-ours* chicken switch."

Hooch glances past Amos's shoulder to see Vera approaching, arms self-embracing across her chest as if to ward off cold. "And what about our humble, elderly diner owners? Do they get a chicken switch too?"

Amos's eyes drift to port. "That I'm still working on…"

"He's dead."

Hooch braces himself belatedly while Amos cages a swallow before turning to face Vera. Her face is wan, the corners of her eyes and mouth tributaries in miniature. Though she'd spoken the words softly, they carried in the space as if blow-horned.

"Damn," Hooch mutters.

"Just now?" Amos prompts.

Vera's mouth parts, but it's Jill who answers from the table, a pensive gaze sheened by tears drifting about the kitchen. "About two hours ago. Didn't want to rouse anybody. He wouldn't have wanted that. One thing Blue despised more than anything was pointlessly interrupted sleep."

"There goes their chicken switch, Doc," Hooch mutters.

Amos fights the scowl he wants to level on everyone. On the world entire. "I'll figure something out."

"Of that, Doc, I have no doubts."

The chortle that ensues from Hooch is too much, and Amos steps again between his parted legs on the stool until their eyes antler. "You think your guns scare me after the things I've seen and done and know? What awaits us?"

"Are you two fucking serious?" Vera says. She moves to pry them apart but relents as soon as she sees Smiles rising to full, menacing height.

"Easy does it, Doc," Hooch says, grinning, surprised and taken by the unexpected chutzpah. The doctor's breath smells harsh and synthetic, like burnt wiring. "Not that I can't handle you solo, but I don't think I'll be able to stop my *cell buddy* should he shift into overkill."

Amos cants eyes at the leisurely approaching Smiles, his damp undershirt vaguely outlining stacked pine-logs of torso muscle, before easing back a step from Hooch. Vera slips in front of him to add an additional buffer, and the unanticipated support puts a quaver in his chest.

"We good?" Smiles asks of nobody in particular, hands clasped behind his back as if to further present the vulnerability of an underside no one sane would dare try taking advantage of.

Hooch is about to level more cheek when an approaching rumble shakes the storefront glass, and moments later a bus, its windows grated over with steel mesh, emerges from stage-right across the windows and stops at the sawhorse barriers, its stubborn momentum dying on a metallic squeal.

"Game time," Hooch says, dismounting his stool and letting a stray shoulder nudge Amos out of the way as he and Smiles quickly get to donning their purloined police costumes.

"I suppose you people have this all planned out to the letter?" Amos says, no longer being subtle with his volume.

Hooch zips up his parka in one sharp pull. "Like you, Doc, we're just making this up as we go. Now listen up. Our esteemed doctor here will carefully and respectfully convey our dearly departed Blue's body to the back, while his two minions get to work fast—and I mean *fast*—to clean that table and the floor around it. Doesn't have to be spotless, just not obviously *Friday the 13th*. Just sop up any still-wet blood, throw a cloth over it, and pile some of those tools over that. Treat it like a workstation. Like most messes, it'll get ignored by the pension-whores aboard that bus."

Amos watches as Smiles is trying to be clandestine in readying several hypodermic needles inside his duffle bag before turning to see both Vera and Doug eyeing him expectantly. With no other alternative or counter-plan in the offing, he just nods at them to heed Hooch's instructions, and he gathers himself before approaching the corner booth and Jill.

"I'm...sorry," he tells her.

She lifts her head from Blue's inert chest. Her eyes stare at nothing. Dabbing a finger on her tongue, she then rubs out the blood smudge on Blue's nose. The action merely rouges it further into his skin. She then reclines into the booth and tips a single nod without eye-contact.

Amos gently hooks his arms under Blue at the shoulders and just below the rump, then hoists him off the table. He's surprisingly light, and only as Amos sets him down on a desk in the back office does he remember from his research that a human leg is nearly 20% of total body weight.

As soon as he returns to the main dining area, he sees Hooch and Smiles doing final checks on their clothing, just as the bus doors outside slide open.

"All right now, everyone assume a breakfast-as-usual position," Hooch says. "And please, no funny business or heroics. Time is long past for that. And besides, in a couple minutes the room will be brimming with guns, and you'll all be sitting between them."

8

HOOCH HEAVES OPEN the door against a bank of snow and the cold punch to the face is a bracing kiss from a beautiful stranger—unexpected, appreciated, and transient, for within ten seconds all he wants is to return to the swelter of the diner. But that's all moot now, and a comparable lax in sharpness made this errand a necessity, and now here he is with Smiles, isolated on a mountain road beset by monsters, to remedy a mistake.

At least the sun winks through, a sliver of gold lukewarmth wriggling through a thick gray pile. If the mad doctor inside is right, it might hold the beasts at bay long enough to free House.

He steps out first, his right hand twitching against his holster, one eye on the tree line and one eye on the bus and the bored, yawning prison guard standing at the door. Behind him, Smiles cheek-welds a department-issued shotgun, sweeping it in controlled arcs to the right where most of the exposed woods lie.

"Morning!" Hooch calls, breaths leaving him as ghosts in flight, all the jovial, country exaggeration he would've otherwise employed as subterfuge swapped out for more pressing stone-cold sobriety.

The prison guard, middle-aged and red-eyed from having babysat a busload of cons during a snowstorm, raises a hand in mechanical salutation. "Morning back. What's with the twenty-one-gun welcome, Officer?"

Hooch stops, with Smiles doing the same a few yards behind, keeping his bores elevated and ready. "You haven't heard?"

The guard squints, muttering blasphemies against a blinding flare of morning sun. "Heard what?"

"On the scanner not ten minutes ago. There's an escaped prisoner out in these woods, considered armed and dangerous."

The guard blinks back his vision, then ducks within the bus to no doubt confab with his cohorts, and at length steps down onto the snow, his boots plunging past their tops to below the knees. "We haven't heard anything, but our scanner's been wonky because of the storm. They say where or how he got out?"

"Transfer from Whitehorse Correctional is all we gathered," Hooch says, stepping up to the guard. The man's breath is two days of plumed coffee and salty, microwaved food. "Likely an accident from the storm in transport. In any case, you're not getting much farther than this diner. Rockslide a quarter-mile down the road. How many you got onboard?"

The guard leans his body at the hip to peer past Hooch at Smiles aiming his weapon at the trees before straightening again. He studies the bald officer before him, his bearing flinty but wary, continuing to dart his eyes between the bus and the woods. "Nice round number of ten," says the guard, smiling wide in an attempt to dissipate the palpable edginess of the two cops. He understands prudence, but one escaped con trudging through sub-freezing temps in only a prison jumper isn't exactly Joint Task Force 2. "Six prisoners, three guards, and a driver." And he sing-songs for additional mirth, "And a partridge in a pear tree..."

His grin falters at the officer's complete disdain at levity.

"Best get everyone inside," Hooch says. "Have some coffee and a nice meal. The poutine is quite good. And like I said, you're not getting down this mountain for a few hours at least."

Once again, the guard performs his pitching-at-the-hip bit, only this time looking at the diner. He makes out a few nondescript heads floating behind the windows. A thin column of smoke coils from a roof vent. Probably an old-fashioned fireplace inside that wouldn't go amiss. He nods and turns to the bus. "Barry?"

A moment later a lean blond guard barely old enough to drink appears at the door cradling a similar shotgun to the one Smiles has trained at the trees. "Yeah, Hal?"

"Bring them out. Road is closed ahead for the next few hours. We'll get some chow while we wait. You take the lead."

Hooch feels all his muscles tighten. "Officer Denton here will take the lead," he says.

The guard—Hal—shrugs. "Eh. Procedure. Glad some still practice the dying art. Hey, Denton? You wouldn't happen to be related to Lonny Denton, would you?"

Smiles barely glances his way before saying, "Cousin."

Hal whistles. "That family sure produces some big boys, all right." He flicks a hand to Barry at the door. "Take the lead. Chris and Del, follow with the driver."

***

"What's happening?" Doug asks.

Amos, who has stationed himself at the booth by the door, watches as the first prisoner in waist and leg shackles carefully steps down onto the snow, shivering noticeably at the new and vicious cold. "Well, it's about to get a lot warmer in here," he says.

"Fucking great," Vera says, pacing before Jill, who continues to stare blankly at the table that only moments earlier held her dead husband.

"Just pray that sun holds," Doug says, sitting at the bar counter. His eyes keep drifting to Smiles' duffle bag, and the guns within it. When he looks back at Amos, Doug sees that he's thinking the same thing.

Amos toggles between Vera and Doug. "Either of you know how to handle a gun?"

Doug embarks on a series of shrugs before yielding to discretion and shaking his head.

"My dad took me to a range a few times," Vera says. "Hunting rifles and six-shooters. Thirty-aught-six Springfield damn near popped out my shoulder."

"It'll do," Amos says, sliding out of the booth and moving quickly to Smiles' bag. A quick rummage, and he comes up with two Walther P99s. He recalls their light weight and smooth, reliable handling in Johannesburg two years earlier, which is all he cares to remember of the episode. Upon checking their clips and safeties, he tucks one against his back beneath his shirt, and quickly takes the other to Vera. "Keep it close but concealed. Just in case."

Vera cups it in both hands as if it were a baby chick before emulating Amos and stuffing it against her back as well.

"Oh shit," manages Amos a split-second before the first scream erupts outside.

***

The young man, Barry, tips his hat in passing Hooch, and the prisoners start filing out behind him.

The fourth one out, a bit grayer at the temples and road-weary in the eyes, but no less physically imposing, is House.

"Don't ever take anything offered to you in here. They'll expect renumeration. That means one or two or up to ten spit-lubed peckers up your mud chute before the guards ever catch wind."

Those had been House's fist words to him upon Hooch refusing the cigarette House offered him in the yard. He would later tell Hooch that he'd falsely assumed him as a first-timer. But Hooch's mother had just died not two days prior, and his head was in the clouds rather than probing the new transfers for threats. House, at least physically, was definitely one of those potential threats. He was massive, as well as an old-timer who surely knew all the games played on the inside.

When Hooch prompted House what he wanted for this unsolicited advice—advice he didn't need, therefore felt no obligation to offer *renumeration*—House took a long drag, then turned wistful and muttered out the corner of his mouth so as not to draw attention.

"Sure, I could fuck you till the cows come home, but I'll work out my own stable here soon enough. Besides, you're not my type. I like long hair on my dogies. In any case, ass is plenty. Skill in the distillation arts, however, is not, and word around here is that you're a master. A renowned talent for righteous toilet booze."

While opting to *not* rape someone wasn't exactly a high bar by which to judge character, Hooch had thought then, that bar rose with time. He and House became fast friends. Favors very quickly became non-transactional—just something to do because no one else would. In a relatively short time, House would confess his fears, his failures, his aspirations to Hooch. He spoke to him as a father would, yet without talking down to him. He readily offered vulnerability. Talked fondly of his younger brother, Smiles, whom he often lamented not having been a better mentor to.

"You should look up Smiles when you get out," he said, a week before Hooch was indeed to be released. *"I think you'd work well together. You have the same problem-solving sense. Same prudence."*

And now, years removed from shared time and, later, shared jobs, he passes Hooch in the snow, batting the same subtle wink with the same frosty gray eyes he always did to signal a conversation's end, and it takes everything in Hooch to fight the impulse to wink back and blow their cover. Despite over a year in prison, the man still smells of old leather and cheap smokes, and Hooch basks in a paternal comfort while under House's brief shadow. It has him thinking of the guard's comment moments ago about the Denton boys being big, though Smiles and House aren't Dentons. But they are dense. So dense that their mother must've thought she was birthing singularities instead of babies.

So lost in reflection is Hooch that it takes him a moment still to realize House's shadow has lingered well beyond him simply having walked by, and his heart picks up as if shot out by starter pistol at realizing why.

The clouds have blotted the sun, and the snarled, *"Fuck,"* from Smiles behind him coincides with the flash of hot blue pinpoints blazing through the brush, and the first foray from the tree line of Outcrosses—half-a-dozen at least charging straight for them just as all the shackled prisoners are exposed in the open, and Smiles unloads his first thundering volley of buckshot.

***

Amos yanks open the door and yells for them to get back inside, but everyone except for Hooch and Smiles is welded to the snow in terror and disbelief at the naked, almost-human things galloping at them on all fours before pouncing almost as one into spread-eagle demon-apparitions of bared claws and teeth.

One has skittered to a stop mere feet from the door before quickly angling for the lead guard. Amos just manages to pull the door shut before the arterial spray slaps the glass.

***

The young guard, Barry, just manages a *"Holy hell?"* before the first Outcross, in a clearly tactical, pre-planned maneuver, de-throats the lead target with a single swipe, cutting off the others from their intended sanctuary.

"House!" Smiles yells, pumping shell after shell into the hurtling blurs dashing into the open, hitting only two—winging one while nearly cleaving a second in half who continues to drag itself several more yards before rolling over dead with a child's disappointed yelp.

Hooch, having temporarily lost House's position, hurdles through the deep snow toward Smiles, firing rapidly but blindly with his sidearm at the advancing beasts, who merely funnel between his wild line of fire and spring upon the prisoners to either side of him trying to make their break for the trees through two feet of snow and against chains that allow for nine-inch strides at best.

Within seconds, limbs and gore fling about the frame of Hooch's vision under a score of shrieks, and only when hot blood mists against the back of his neck does his momentary paralysis break. He starts powering again through deep snow for the diner, anticipating that House would do the same. He looks back in time to see the two trailing guards get ribboned by talons to the ground, one while in a futile kneel in the snow to draw better aim, the other while trying to make it back to the bus, only to get cut down at the steps, an Outcross shearing away his arm at the shoulder still gripping to the handrail.

All throughout, as terror and mission-urgency duke it out for dominance in his gut, Hooch can hear their unnerving strain between the victims' screams and the panic-pants of his own breaths. Their prepubescent grunts and exertions as they hack their prey to more easily conveyable portions, as if rough-and-tumbling in a playground or griping while trudging through boring chores.

He's jolted back to the moment as Smiles nearly collides into him, running in the opposite direction, heading for the bus. Hooch is about to question where he's going when it hits him: in his blind lumbering run back for the sanctuary of the diner, he overshot House—House, who is now swinging the severed leg of another prisoner to stave off the coiling forms of two Outcrosses crouched to either side of him.

The same panic, he realizes, that he felt before abandoning House during a bungled job now over two years old. And as if catching onto that very wavelength, House narrows his eyes on Hooch, and despite not understanding the nature of the creatures he's trying to stave off with purloined body parts, he flicks a backhand his way.

Get out of here, the gesture says.

Someone plows into his shoulder, turning him nearly a perfect three-sixty, before realizing it's Smiles running toward his brother. Smiles bellows back at him to man the diner door before arcing down his now-empty shotgun atop the head of the nearest Outcross. It stuns the beast enough for Smiles to continue pummeling it to a pulp with his otherwise useless weapon.

For a blink of time, Hooch feels compelled to help, the call to redemption yodeling as a rapidly fading echo in his head. But the brothers, though they love and accept him, also know that he's the weak link. The first to hesitate and even bolt at the apex of chaos. He's glimpsed it in their mutual, head-cocked, melancholy gazes directed his way, as if he were the runt of a litter perpetually last to the teat. And while Hooch's mind has always *thought* action, his body always held other opinions, and all fancies of deliverance are promptly choked by the exigencies of life-and-limb reality as the Outcross before House parries easily a fumbling, clumsy backswing of leg before springing onto its target while momentum has its prey all turned around.

House roars his agony—a sound too close to his raucous, joyous belly-laughs at bawdy jokes and completed jobs—and Hooch's legs pivot and drive him back toward the diner, splashing unknowingly into a pool of blood still pumping from Barry's body, looking back only after Amos pushes out the door to let him in.

Smiles is still some fifty feet back, slogging toward the diner, a hand dragging his brother along by his jumpsuit's collar while House swings blindly back with another severed limb. An arm this time, and it takes Hooch a moment to understand that it's House's own freshly shorn arm he's windmilling behind himself with his still intact arm. And he actually manages a solid *thunk* on the head of the pursuing Outcross with his detached elbow before it shudders off the impact and leaps on House's back, sending him face-first into the parking lot snow already mottled in deep-red lagoons.

Smiles gawks at the seditious hand up close that was seconds earlier holding onto his brother before he turns and leaps onto the back of the Outcross already two-hand unzipping House's spinal cord from his madly snow-angeling body.

"Smiles!" Hooch screams, struggling against Amos, who's trying to bear-hug him inside.

But it's to no avail. Three Outcrosses rush in from three different directions, scrambling for traction in the snow before acquiring enough to steady and spring onto Smiles and House.

Hooch, still shouting, draws his second sidearm and empties the clip wildly in their general direction, missing thrashing Outcross and carved laps of flesh and unspooling entrails alike before the combined forces of Amos, Vera, and Doug manage at last to haul Hooch inside and lock the door.

***

Seething spittle and befuddled panic, Hooch lunges for the door again, screaming for Smiles and House, and once more the three scientists have to put their all into holding him back before he relents at last in a limp, hitching, blubbering mess that Amos feels an instant, unfamiliar compulsion to corral and embrace.

"I'm sorry," he whispers into Hooch's ear, and Hooch grumbles similar apologies to his fallen brothers outside currently being pared and scattered amongst six Outcrosses who ferry their respective plunder quickly into the woods.

"Jesus, Jill," Vera says, her calm but succinct voice a champagne flute being tapped before a speech.

Doug swallows and takes a step toward Jill, but she flicks on her lighter, freezing everyone in place.

Because the red plastic gas can now rolls in a slow half-circle at her feet, and soon the entire room wafts of pungent gasoline sheeting down the storefront glass and dappling the orange vinyl of the booths and tabletops.

Dripping down Jill's very hair and clothing.

Hooch, having torn his eyes from outside and taken in the new predicament, sweeps Amos away with one arm while holding out his other hand at Jill.

"Please," he says, his eyes swinging between what's left of Smiles and House outside, and another undeserving soul now set to die on his watch. "What…will this gain you?"

Her pupils etch the tiny flame flickering in her hand. "Forgetting," she tells the fire, then looks up at the foursome before her. "I think you should all leave now. Our Forester's out back. Tires are chained. Keys are hanging by the back door."

"We'll *all* go," Vera says. She takes a slow step forward, and Jill mirrors the action by moving the lighter closer to her chest.

"Okay, Jill," Amos says, drawing Vera back. "We'll go."

"The fuck we will," Hooch says. The words are weakly chewed and dribbled rather than spat, but the smolder in his eyes remains undeniable.

Amos turns and edges himself between Hooch and Jill. "Take her car and get Doug and Vera out of here. I'll get Jill out on the bus."

"Asshole, we're not leaving you," Vera cuts in.

"You and Doug have to resolve this, especially if I don't make it. This is your best chance—right now while we have some sun and the Outcrosses have been…sated."

Vera's eyes bore into his, beating wide and damp in their sockets all the umbrages, terror, and appeals that words can't. Perhaps only action can with the man whose child she carries, unbeknownst to him, and heeding to this sudden whim, she draws the very pistol Amos handed her and points it at his heart. "No more fucking debating. You're coming."

Amos heaves a long breath, then steps forward until the muzzle and sight dimples the flesh of his chest. Their eyes entwine. It's a connection they've always denied in the lab, and sometimes even out of it, for it left them defenseless against stranding upon unfamiliar shores with new climates and languages to adapt to. She always seemed more willing to learn, especially of late, and now her trembling scowl is a lasso flung and pulled taut across his chest, hoping to lure him to dry sand.

"You *will* have to shoot me," he says. "You know that, right? And unlike what's happened here, that's a crime you'll have to own one hundred percent."

The gun starts to tremor, and for a moment Amos prepares himself. She's *going* to shoot, either unintentionally through panic or purposely through betrayal, and he relaxes against this inevitability. There's undeniable solace in knowing it's from someone he cares about and shares mutual respect with. He always figured it would come from the far longer list of people who despised him. And as he pictures the bullet obliterating his heart and turning out his lights for good, he feels the gun slide down his chest.

He opens his eyes to Doug gently nudging Vera toward the kitchen. Even walking backwards, she clutches her belly as if to stymie vomit, her eyes tear-rimed and still clasped to Amos's.

"Asshole," she whispers, and as Doug keeps pulling her away, all the guilt she's amassed at keeping the pregnancy from Amos puddles behind her.

Hooch breaks their staring contest by stepping before Amos.

"You get her out, Doc," he says, thumbing at Jill, the menace and threat back in his voice.

Amos glances over his shoulder. "You just remember what we talked about. We've all got the same hands in the same cookie jar. You get them to safety, then you go your own way and you don't look back."

The wry, sad grin Hooch levels is capitulation enough for Amos, and as Hooch follows Doug and Vera to the back, he angles himself toward Jill, pausing long enough to whisper, "It's Robert, and I truly am sorry," before moving on.

Once gone, both Jill and Amos's eyes coast together. The flat, cold light of inexorability tethers their gazes, their thoughts in harmonic resonance, simply because there's nowhere else to go, nothing more to be done.

At length Jill turns and walks casually back to the booth, lit lighter still flickering perilously close to her chest.

Just as nonchalantly, Amos draws his pistol from his back and aims it between her shoulder blades. With Blue gone, so is her plausible chicken switch. They kept each other honest and moving forward, and now that engine is stalled for good.

Is this how she'd want it? he ponders. The coldness of a stranger's execution? Or should her own hand do the honors?

The debate continues to oscillate, even as he watches her drag out Blue's shotgun from the booth that, at some point during the bus attack, she found space and wherewithal to reacquire unseen. Or maybe they had a second shotgun stashed away nearby—one that maybe only she knew about and kept from Blue, like her cigarettes. Amos would never put that past her, and he now understands Hooch's poorly concealed admiration for the woman.

This is, after all, *her* place.

She squares up with Amos at a distance, showing no surprise at seeing him leveling a gun at her. Her own weapon rests against her chest, the one hand with the still lit lighter nestled against the fore-end slide, and the other wrapping the grip, finger nestled against the trigger.

From out back roars to life an engine, followed by the gravel-wash of snow being kicked up by tires.

Jill's melancholy smile doles out equal beauty and regret, and she says, "It's time," right before pulling the trigger.

The glass above the corner booth they all sat in today, and where a kindly old man later bled to death, blows out in a crater a split-second before the rest of the pane tinkles down in a waterfall of tempered glass cubes.

The vacating heat tussles immediately with the invading cold, churning a sudden but brief vortex above the table, swirling tools and bloody tablecloth into a conical heap.

All the heat rapidly slipstreams out of the diner like the air in a fuselage during sudden decompression, flaring then blowing out the already dying embers of the fire in the Hibachi.

Jill reaches casually behind her—to the coat tree against the booth—and lobs to Amos his parka. It lands at his feet, and as he bends to pick it up, he hears the click-grind of the Bic as she restrikes her snuffed lighter.

They share a final look as he pulls on and zips up his jacket. While no camaraderie twinkles in their stares, there's no enmity either. Only a passing *this-could've-gone-better* lamentation.

Amos nods once, then moves to the door and, upon seeing no fervent, arctic eyes in the trees, pushes out and starts for the bus, gun drawn and sweeping before him. He looks down enough to sidestep steaming puddles of gore and to avoid tripping on unidentifiable torsos the Outcrosses will soon return for. He'd programmed them not to leave anything behind. No waste whatsoever. The nascent and revolutionary DNA reprogramming he'd been hired to investigate and, if possible, implement.

He pauses as the sound of an engine revs nearby, then spots the nose of an SUV peeking out from the corner of the diner before suddenly flooring it, a fan of muddy snow waking behind it. As the vehicle half-donut-spins and at last rumbles onto the highway, he sees why the sudden bolting: two Outcrosses have jumped onto the roof and anchored themselves to the sheet metal. They shimmy in a mutual side-to-side dance as the diminishing SUV tries to slalom them off before disappearing around the next bend.

Amos raises his pistol for all the good it would do, and as his heart revs up in his chest he makes a dash for the bus. His intention had been to drive it in the opposite direction to lead the Outcrosses away, and now he's gauging if there's enough turn-radius in the small parking lot to swing the bus around in pursuit.

A whoosh of dense heat nearly sends him sprawling face-first into the snow, and when he looks back he sees the corner of the diner engulfed in flames. Through the shattered pane, he watches the single, unmoving column of fire that was once Jill hold fast for shockingly long seconds before finally crumpling out of view.

The stench, however familiar and muted by the cold, still hits his nostrils moments later, and it impels him forward, if for nothing else than to outrun his rising gorge.

Taking the steps up the bus, he slips twice on blood pools and nearly wipes out before righting himself and seeing what he dreaded: there is no key in the ignition.

He quickly checks the sun visor. Also nothing.

The keys are still on the driver.

He steps to the door and searches a vigorously disturbed snow divoted by footfall and drenched in slaughter—but which torso is the driver's? He never got a good look at him, aside from a quick glimpse of salt-and-pepper hair that implied age.

Except there are no heads left to match the bodies.

A distant but unmistakable impact, followed by the closer squawks of startled birds.

Despite the amorphous source of the crash dying now as an echo, Amos knows from where it stemmed. Down the road where the SUV had sped off. He stares eastward, hand gripped to the boarding rail as the silence of the woods soon regains dominance.

And then the quick, muffled pops of faraway pistol reports, followed seconds later by a quickly rising female scream that gets abruptly cut off at its apex.

"Vera..." Amos mouths.

Back to silence, and when Amos tears his eyes at last from the highway, they land upon the lone upright Outcross standing but a few feet before the bus steps.

Switches of blood pepper its face and bare skull. Its arms, however, from elbows to flexing fingers, are saturated in it, as if its skin had been turned inside-out.

It cants its head at Amos. An inquiring coo seeps from its mouth.

Amos's gun hand drops to his side. All of his air furls out in a single spectral column the wind takes for its own.

"Saul?" he whispers.

***

The Outcross's stout muzzle flares slightly, pushing forth something resembling a grin. *Smile* lives in its eyes, however, cerulean and pulsing like starlight. Somehow the specific human trait survived in the alpha. The soft brow-curve meeting in a harsh cavity above the nose.

Exactly like his mother.

So rapt by the undeniability of his reforged son before him, he at first fails to notice the other glacial eyes appearing in the tree line, acknowledging them only after Saul snaps a quick bark in both directions.

Hold fast.

And then the gesture that nearly cleaves Amos's heart in two: Saul half-turning and waving with a limp, bloody wrist for him to follow. A perfect child's gesture.

Amos's fingers flex and individually re-grip around the gun before stepping off the bus. At the crunch of his footfalls on snow, almost like a trigger, a low, rumbling grouse issue from the concealed Outcrosses that Saul has to once more check with a growl. He looks back at Amos periodically as he skulks toward the trees, verifying that he's following.

That *Dad* is behind him.

A more emphatic *come-hither* wave at Amos and a curt squeak.

Get close and stay close.

Despite the fear icing his bones and squatting at the top of his throat in a burning lump, Amos abides, moving to within feet of the creature. Its bone-gray back is corded in lean, lethal muscle that twists and distends with every step, every breath. Its smell, less potent outside than within a sterile control room, is the puff of new, freshly opened electronic components, now augmented by the unmistakable tang of blood.

But the back of his head. His nubbin ears and their precise jut. What he saw as he patted his back whenever he choked during a bottle feeding.

Suddenly he turns, hearing seconds before Amos a distant revving of engine, before retraining his eyes to the trees.

Maybe one or two of them made it, he thinks. But which one or two?

He follows Saul. Behind him, the Last Chance Grill burns bright for the last time.

***

As they proceed into the trees and the light darkens precipitously, the rustle and snap of nearby foliage follows them close to either side, the silhouettes of shadowing Outcrosses hardly distinguishable from the total darkness beyond.

A shiver jolts through Amos's limbs, though whether from the fresh cold or mounting dread, he wouldn't dare wager on. He's in pure hunting grounds now. No more open spaces for visual advantage, no more climate-controlled bubbles as barriers, but perfect concealment for leisurely dismemberment and devouring.

They walk through pristine, powdered snow for a good ten minutes, the world a latticework of blues and blacks and cheek-sizzling ice. As Amos rubs his arms in vain efforts to warm up, Saul continues unperturbed, head on a swivel, his body fully acclimated as designed, storing surplus heat from augmented calorie burn in cold weather.

To either side, just out of sight, Outcrosses chitter and whine, their winging stretching to a crescendo just as he and Saul reach the entrance of a cave.

The opening is a narrow, jagged pyramid barely as high as an adult, fissured at the base of a granite rise.

Saul palms the edges of the opening and inhales long and deep. Amos sees other handprints along the rock captured in various stages of dried blood, suggesting this as Saul's routine.

His ritual.

He looks over his shoulder, and in one head-to-toe undulation, beckons Amos in before ducking through himself.

***

Saul's eyes.

Their glow is all Amos has for illumination, and even then, he feels his pupils dilated to their limits to drink in every available photon. Every other step is a near stumble on crag or trough of rock. The cold is bitter, searching, alive in its malice. The air is stagnant with moisture, and a cloying sweetness beneath. The hint of spoilage.

At one point, as if sensing Amos's struggles, Saul reaches back and clamps his hand around his father's wrist as guide, his elongated fingers nearly double-orbiting the wrist.

His grip is firm—tight but not painful. Dare Amos conjecture, even *loving*?

Gradually the light ahead increases, as do sounds of juvenile vocalizing and…eating?

The sweetness in the air has been replaced by the dampness of old standing water and boiling meat, the iciness of the temperature notwithstanding.

As the space brightens, so does the passage's breadth widen, and in his periphery, Amos spots Outcrosses crouched within rock niches, gnawing away at human limbs he'd rather not dwell on, and who pause abruptly their chewing and extend their necks his way at his surprising presence.

One by one they drop their vulgar cuts and follow, noses snuffling, mouths grumbling inquiry and growls, which Saul rebuffs with heartier snarls.

The opening high on the cavern wall nearly blinds Amos, so unexpected its potency despite only casting cold, clouded-over light. Yet it works as crude oculus for a spacious cavern as wide as a tennis court.

Outcrosses, eye-smolder somewhat muted by the bright-washed walls, rise to full height from whatever occupied them at seeing their leader followed by a man. Followed by prey that by all accounts should not have entered their sanctuary on its own power. And as if by osmosis, the same notion slips into Amos as well, though the sight of the place is its own statement of fact.

Limbs stripped of footwear and clothing lean along the curved walls for half the circumference of the space, whatever blood not drained living as frozen black smears the stumps have airbrushed into the stone against which they rest. In the middle of the space humps a bloody, tattered pile of clothing and ribcages, the later still glistening from whatever fresh flesh or saliva the bones still grip to.

He sees it then in their hands. Naturally, being at highest and fastest risk of spoilage, organs and viscera would be the first things they'd have to consume.

At the foot of the heap, spaced out like ramparts, the eyeless heads of their spoils that Amos averts from before recognition can grease his knees into giving out.

Saul turns and stands before him, shoulders reeled back, chest high and heaving. On his right thigh, the little amoeba-shaped mole his mother referred to as his spirit mark. Below his left elbow, the little scar from tumbling onto gravel while learning to ride his bike.

Amos traces this scar as Saul's arms rise to either side in a gesture of bestowal.

He's showing what he's made.

Showing his father.

This is what he conditioned them to do, and what he feared would pass through in his own boy: pride and vanity in wholesale carnage.

The others chirrup and trill in their high, immature timbres as a new group of their pack enters the space then, slowing in wonder at seeing the interloper.

Their maker.

Under their arms are clutched freshly dismembered limbs. In one is a head, and Amos is too slow to look away before registering Hooch's bald, bloody dome.

His eyes stumble back to Saul. The last time he beheld him standing was before the leukemia had cut him down at fourteen, already balding from treatment and brittle as a newborn foal despite having inherited his father's height. The coma followed shortly, then the pronouncement of mere days to go by the oncologist. He convinced Diana to sign the DNR. By then she'd moved out to her parents, speaking to Amos only regarding their child.

The signed death certificate, coupled with Amos's transfer to Alaska on a government project soon thereafter, splintered their marriage for good.

Saul *had* died—the pronouncement made in the ICU—but his little heart kicked back on again minutes later, and with it, Amos's resolution to act. His DNA work, while nascent, was already showing remarkable promise, above and beyond estimates, and it could save him. Save his boy. Soon prudence gave way to possibility, possibility to practice, practice to perfection.

Love to accomplishment.

And now, almost three years later, here stood the fruits of his headlong, singular rush. Here stood not only his recovered boy, but all his salvaged children, none of which he asked for, and none of whom had asked for his rescue, but only for nurture and a fair shot at meaning.

The Outcrosses have all migrated behind Saul, just over a dozen in total. They flank him like bannermen, like lieutenants, each naked yet equally deadly.

Then Saul advances.

He stops mere feet from Amos, his neck craning to match his father's eyes.

And Amos, who already struggles to keep his knees locked, allows himself to sag enough to match Saul's eye level, and a blubber shoots out of him he tries too late to block with a hand.

"I'm so sorry, Saul," he says through splayed fingers. "I tried…to make you stronger. Stronger than me. But my weakness… That's what made you. Not my…"

Other words swirl in Amos's mind, other apologies, other regrets, other promises both gone and salvageable, and when his mouth parts to allow one to make itself known, it snaps shut instantly at recognizing with mounting horror what is happening. What should not be happening.

Saul, against all programming and discretion to his own wellbeing, starts kneeling before his father and extends an open hand.

He's supplicating.

"No, no," Amos says, taking Saul's wrist and trying to raise him back up. But Saul is strong. So incredibly strong and unyielding, and behind him the Outcrosses yelp first confusion, then growl indignation—a trait Amos never thought to deprogram, or even could if he'd considered it in advance.

Traits that, for better or worse, and like many others, are too deeply encoded to alter.

"Get up, Saul!" he hisses, his panic hot in the frigid cave.

The nearest Outcross, likely the one most apt to challenge his leadership status, scurries forward and slashes its talons across Saul's side.

Saul grunts as four perfect welts furrow and split open across his ribs. But he doesn't budge, he doesn't rise.

"Get up, Saul!" Amos hollers.

Two other Outcrosses spring forward, each likewise slashing one-two Saul's back before quickly retreating.

Amos draws his gun and roars at the pack, but the pack all narrow their phosphorescent eyes not on him, but Saul.

At his weakness. At his betrayal.

But all Amos can focus on are Saul's eyes, their sparkle growing like twin suns about to supernova. A pair of tears stream down his gray cheeks, and the salt of this expulsion stirs the Outcrosses into a frenzy, and like water from a blown dam, they deluge upon Saul, who refuses to yield his anchorage, even as the pack starts tearing him apart.

Fury, grief, and bullets fire from Amos, the rapid and reloaded shots exploding skulls, showering blood, dispensing light that travels down the tunnel from which he'd entered. The strobes vaguely register in the eyes of the wildlife that have ventured close to its opening, drawn by the mineral stench of fresh kill, and the bedlam from the mountain's womb winds through the trees and rises beyond their reach, where they're swallowed by clouds roaring back their own newborn thunder across these remote and ephemeral lands.

ACKNOWLEDGMENTS

Heartfelt thanks to my ever-reliable support group of steadfast friends and family who regularly try coaxing information about new work on the horizon without being too demanding or pushy. Writing is hard work that tends to follow its own schedule no matter how hard we try to squeeze it into the precious few hours or even minutes at our disposal. Special thanks to my growing tribe of fellow writers, both in-the-flesh and online, not the least of which being the Secret Sexy Horror Discord (Eli, Kathryn, Lisa, and Mackenzie)—amazing friends and MFAs who've adopted this stray, non-MFA pooch into their midst.

ABOUT THE AUTHOR

Dino Parenti is a writer of dark, speculative fiction. Author of the Imadjinn Award Finalist short-fiction collection, *Dead Reckoning and Other Stories,* he also won the first annual *Lascaux Review* flash fiction contest and was featured in the Anthony Award winning anthology *Blood on the Bayou.* He lives in Los Angeles.